ᚠᛁᚲᛁᚿᚵ ᚦᚢᛖᛋᛏ

# Viking Quest

## Tom Henighan

An imprint of
Beach Holme Publishing
Vancouver

Copyright © 2001 by Tom Henighan

First Edition

This book is published by Beach Holme Publishing, 226–2040 West 12th Avenue, Vancouver, B.C. V6J 2G2. This is a Sandcastle Book.

The publisher gratefully acknowledges the financial support of the Canada Council for the Arts and of the British Columbia Arts Council. The publisher also acknowledges the financial assistance received from the Government of Canada through the Book Publishing Industry Development Program (BPIDP) for its publishing activities.

The Canada Council | Le Conseil des Arts
for the Arts | du Canada

BRITISH
COLUMBIA
ARTS COUNCIL
Supported by the Province of British Columbia

Editor: Michael Carroll
Production and Design: Jen Hamilton
Cover Art: Ljuba Levstek
Author Photograph: Marilyn Carson

Printed and bound in Canada by Webcom

**National Library of Canada Cataloguing in Publication Data**

Henighan, Tom.
 Viking quest

 "A Sandcastle book."
 ISBN 0-88878-421-X

 I. Title.
PS8565.E582V5 2001      jC813'.54      C2001-910124-4
PZ7.H3875Vi 2001

ᚼᚱᛏᚼᛈᛕᚼᛏᛁᛏᛏᛁ

# Acknowledgements

I would like to thank George Johnston for sending me his translation of *The Saga of the Greenlanders* (Porcupine's Quill, 1994), which I referred to frequently while I was writing this story. Another book constantly at hand was Farley Mowat's provocative and fascinating *Westviking* (McClelland & Stewart, 1965). For fictional purposes I have adopted Mowat's speculation that Trinity Bay, Newfoundland, may have been the real location of Vinland, even though there is no evidence to prove it. In my narrative I have tried to render accurately both the history and natural history of medieval Newfoundland, even though I have freely invented details where it seemed useful and appropriate to do so. For example, I have included animals, such as white-tailed deer, groundhogs, and frogs, that some scientists argue did not exist on the island at that time.

My thanks to my friends Pam and Mark Graydon and their children Laura and Pierce, and to my former student Gerardo Barajas Garrido, who were a wonderful first audience—intelligent, helpful, informed, and enthusiastic. The gifted students of my wife Marilyn's Ottawa elementary-school class read this book in manuscript, corrected my spelling, raised a myriad of interesting questions, learned the runes, and thrilled me with their imaginative projects relating to the story. I must also thank Bill Milliken, who made it possible for me to take a two-day voyage on a Viking replica ship—the experience was memorable and instructive.

I owe a debt of gratitude to Michael Carroll of Beach Holme Publishing for his interest in my work and for his great expertise in editing, publishing, and marketing. Without his encouragement this book would never have been written.

Finally, I want to dedicate this book to Owen and Hugh Powell, two of my young friends who live in Yorkshire, England, one of the former Viking lands. I hope they and all my young readers grow up to live (and possibly write) their own sagas of adventure.

This is the forest primeval. The murmuring pines and the hemlock
Bearded with moss, and in garments green, indistinct in the twilight...
Loud from its rocky caverns, the deep-voiced neighbouring ocean
Speaks, and in accents disconsolate answers the wail of the forest.

—Henry Wadsworth Longfellow, *Evangeline*

# Prologue

Long before he became a man, Rigg had much to remember. His father, impressed by what the boy had seen and done, would sometimes ask him to tell his own story of Vinland—to recite, in the fashion of a *skald*, or poet, his great adventure.

They would sit by the home fire, in true Viking fashion, sharing a cup of mead or wine, and Rigg would tell his story. Of course, he did not tell everything: what son tells his father everything? And if his father is a hero and a famous man, perhaps his son tells him even less.

Leif Eriksson was a famous man. Hearing of the existence of the great and fertile islands to the west, Leif had sailed from Greenland, basing his navigation on what Bjarni Herjolfsson had reported of the sightings and currents. Bjarni, an Icelander and a very skilled navigator, was a man of few words. Trying to sail to Greenland to find his own father, he had been blown off course and had discovered this wonderful new land, some parts of it rich and fertile with trees and grasslands.

Bjarni had not landed, but his descriptions were detailed. Leif had taken note and had made the crossing a few years later. He had actually landed in the new country, claiming the land as his own, taking off much timber and wintering over in a small lagoon well protected from the sea. Tyrkir, a German who had nursed Leif in his youth, had wandered off one day and had found wild grapes and vines and berries in abundance, and Leif had called the new country Vinland.

In the spring, when he decided to sail back to Greenland, Leif asked if any of his party were courageous enough to wait for him in Vinland. He planned to return in the fall, he explained, and to load up enough ships to make his fortune in timber and animal skins. He did not insist that any of his men stay, knowing the dangers that might threaten them, but asked for volunteers.

The first to volunteer was Ivar, a powerful fighter, stern and taciturn, but very brave and resourceful. The second was Rolf, a clever man, skilled in handicrafts, and a good sailor. A few others also agreed to stay, since Leif promised them extra shares of the land and profits.

Then, to Leif's surprise, his own natural son Rigg, the child of the Irish woman Fianna, also volunteered. Leif laughed, slapped the boy on the shoulder, and told him it was impossible. He had great affection for Rigg, a tall ungainly lad of fifteen, and had some secret fears about how well those left behind would fare. But when Rigg insisted, Leif agreed to consider the matter, and a few days later—to everyone's surprise—he finally gave his assent. Perhaps the experience would make a man of the boy, he decided, for Rigg was far too dreamy and lost in his own thoughts; he seemed afraid of violence and shied away from the rough jokes of the Viking sailors. No one knew exactly what kind of man he would become and Leif, who believed that the action makes the man, decided the boy should stay behind and learn from his new experiences.

At the same time Leif knew it took courage to volunteer, and he was too wise a father to discourage his son by rejecting such a gesture. He did, however, make the condition that Tyrkir the German should also stay behind. In the absence of Erik the Red, Rigg's real grandfather, Tyrkir proved a kind of foster father to the boy, as he had been to Leif himself.

Leif was surprised, however, when Fianna, Rigg's mother, insisted that she, too, would stay behind. At first Leif resisted, but Fianna, although Irish, was as willful as any Norse woman, and soon had her way. It had occurred to Leif that she would be a good influence on the boy and balance what the fighting men would teach him, and besides, Leif was a little tired of her superior ways. She was a clever woman, skilled in the arts of healing and familiar with much traditional lore, but she could sometimes be hard to deal with. Leif knew the voyage back to Greenland would be more restful without her and was not sorry she wanted to stay behind with Rigg.

It might have appeared that Leif had thought things out carefully, had planned well, and understood the situation, but that was not altogether true. For Leif did not know what was in his son's heart, nor did he know anything about the dreams, visions, and experiences the boy had already had in the new land.

Rigg had not volunteered to stay behind in Vinland for any reason that Leif, the man of action, would understand. The boy had asked to stay behind because the new land had already marked him, dazzled him, with visions of things strange and mysterious. Somewhere, perhaps in the deepest heart of those endless forests, the boy hoped to find living things, or traces of the past, or unsuspected treasures—wonders that would burst on him and shed a new light on everything, on his own life, on the world of the Vikings, even on nature itself. Rigg, it seemed, was in search of some magic essence of life he could hardly have described, even to his mother. When he watched Leif and his ships sail away one spring morning, disappearing around the low hills at the far end of the vast fjord where they had landed, it was with sadness. But he also felt hopeful that now at last something wonderful, something unique and unforgettable, would burst upon him and change his life forever.

# The Thing in the Forest

Rigg clambered up the old maple, took hold of a sturdy branch, and swung himself in toward the massive trunk. He moved quickly, his heart beating fast. He was confident and quick and felt himself a match for any beast, even the shambling thing he had seen approaching down the forest path. Still, he was wary.

Using the branches as laddered steps, he climbed into the leafy world so different from everything he had known in the old country, the place of his birth, Greenland. There glaciers streaked the bare mountains, the sea crashed on jagged cliffs: that was an open country, full of wind and light. Here, in the new land, darkness clung to the earth, and great forests spread beyond the clear spaces of the shore. Who could guess what lay in the heart of such forests? Trolls or dragons, some said, or werewolves—beings whom spear or axe could not harm and who could change shape at will—or giants worse than any in the old stories.

Rigg believed in such creatures, although he had never seen one, but he knew that a more likely threat would come from quite different animals, from the great bears that haunted these woods, one of whom had just lumbered by on the path below; from the wild boar in the thicket; from the great fish that lurked off the shore; from the thundering herds of caribou that could trample a man into the dust.

Even if Ivar, their chieftain, had not warned him to stay close to the shore he would not have ventured very far into these woods. It was an honour for a boy of fifteen—even for the son of Leif Eriksson—to be allowed to stand watch for the Viking encampment, and Rigg was eager to prove his skill. He was well aware that Ivar, a ferocious warrior, did not altogether trust him.

Not a tall man but lithe and powerful in body, with dark eyes and short-clipped hair and beard, Ivar stood out among the shaggy Vikings. Rigg was a little afraid of this man, who made him think of a big, dangerous cat. And no matter what the subject, they seldom understood each other.

From childhood Rigg had learned how to wield sword and axe, but the idea of killing repelled him. The boy was good at watching, listening, at reading signs and portents. He was happiest in the water or climbing trees; he loved the old stories, or hearing about dreams and portents. Ivar had scornfully told Leif himself that Rigg was more like the son of a priest than the offspring of a chief. At this Leif had laughed, winked at his son, and said to Ivar, "The youngster may surprise you yet. Just be sure you let him off the leash, as I've done!"

Leif's word was law, and so Rigg was given guard duty and full responsibility as a man. Yet even now he knew he had strayed too far into the woods, thus violating Ivar's specific orders. And there was good reason for those orders.

This forest was impossible to navigate, endless, a great trap. Birches shot up around him, also spruce and fir. In the distance he could see tamarack and great elms. The sunlight only emphasized the dark greens of the impenetrable bush. Here everything was a tangle, the paths mere animal trails. The Vikings had no love of this place.

Rigg climbed higher to where the branches thinned out. He swung his lanky body upward, pushed the leaves apart, and peered seaward. What he saw was reassuring. He could make out the broad reaches of the fjord and part of the curving shore. A trail of smoke rose from the Viking encampment, but he could not actually see the top of the booth, or main house.

He rested a while on his high perch, waiting for the scent of the bear to dissipate, listening for the birds' subdued chatter to resume its carefree note. From the way the sunlight slanted through the thick leaf canopy, the boy knew it was late afternoon and that he ought to be getting back to his post. There was a slight chill in the air, a chill the Vikings had first felt about a week ago.

The blazing heat of midsummer was gone now, and every evening the Vikings would wrap themselves tighter in their skin cloaks and build their fires a little higher. The year was moving on; months had passed since Leif's ship had left with the timber. Leif had promised he would try to return from Greenland before the winter with more ships and men. Their leader was a great navigator, but nothing was certain on the great and treacherous ocean lake that stretched all the way to Greenland and Iceland and to old Europe beyond. Ships had disappeared and men nearly as skilled as Leif had perished in storms and shipwrecks. The Viking settlers knew better than to spend their days scanning the horizon. They cut wood for timber and also for their own *knarr*, or seagoing cargo ship, which they had started to build in case Leif did not return. They stocked food, explored a little, kept watch, and cast nervous glances at the deep woods.

The Vikings had come through one winter safe and sound, but then Leif and the others had been with them. Now there were only eighteen settlers left, one of them a woman.

Rigg had sensed the increasing anxiety of the Viking leaders. Ivar himself seemed unnerved by the lack of activity, by the endless waiting. He had tightened the rules of the camp and put everyone on notice to be ready, as if he feared some terrible danger might be in the offing.

Two watches and an extra spell of wood-cutting had been given to Rigg. Even now he was supposed to be on guard, not in the woods, but at a post they had set in a small hillock some miles inland from the camp. There was a horn there, tied to a tree stump, to be used to alert the camp. No one dared imagine what might cause the horn to be sounded.

Now, snug as he was in the tree, Rigg knew he ought to be getting back. Slowly, hand over hand, he descended. When he came down to the broad, thick lower branches, he paused, peering through the leafy canopy, balancing himself, his gaze fixed on the creature that stood in the path some thirty feet below.

What he saw startled him. The bear that had caused him to scamper up the tree was gone, and in its place stood a fine antlered deer with head held high and strong back muscles visibly twitching in the tension of waiting and watching.

It was a common animal, but exactly like one Rigg had recently dreamed of. In his dreams it had been a magic deer and had led him through the woods to a cave, dark and mysterious, one that had turned out to be full of treasure.

Sharing the treasure with the Vikings, Rigg had become a famous chief like his father. Old Tyrkir had helped him remember that dream. They had cast the runes to understand it better. At that point Rigg had recalled another part of the dream: there was something frightening, something unknown and terrifying in the cave. He must have escaped it, but he could not remember how. Nor could he remember the nature of the evil thing.

The deer moved slightly, its nostrils quivering. Rigg drew his long knife and waited.

Minutes passed. The deer known to Rigg were not all dream animals. The previous winter the boy had helped Leif kill a couple of real caribou, and he enjoyed the taste of venison. He imagined himself dropping onto the creature's back and slaying it on the spot. He would be a hero; the whole camp would welcome this cache of fresh meat. Had the animal been sent by the gods or the fates so that he might prove himself as a hunter? Or had his dream-deer come to life to lead him to a treasure? What would Leif expect of him here?

Rigg soon dismissed the idea of trying to kill the deer. He knew that if he attempted a leap from this height he might break an arm or a leg. It would not be easy to fell a deer in this forest, and to get the carcass back to camp might be impossible. Besides, he did not want to kill the deer; it was a splendid and sensitive animal. The Vikings had plenty of food—at least for now. And what if the deer was not a deer at all but the enchanted creature of his dreams? No, this was an animal to follow and not to kill.

Rigg replaced his knife, and as he did so, the deer sprang away and disappeared into the thicket. The boy slid roughly from branch to branch and dropped lightly onto the turf. He knew he would have to follow the animal at least a little way into the woods.

Before shinnying up the tree he had hung his small axe—a gift from Tyrkir—on one of the lower branches of the old maple. He had done so with some reluctance for the sake of an easy climb, and now he was glad once again to feel the weight and heft of his weapon. Clasping the axe tightly in his right hand, he moved cautiously forward, peering at the track, pushing the scrub bush apart, steeling himself against the panic that threatened to send him scurrying back the way he had come.

The woods looked beautiful in the shimmering sunlight, but Rigg wondered what might be hidden behind the screening leaves, the thick trunks, what might lurk in the hollows and beyond the scattered boulders on this faintly trodden track.

The land had begun to slope up, and he reasoned he would soon reach a point from which he could get some kind of view and take stock of how far he had come beyond the bare hillock where the Vikings had staked out the guard post. He knew he must get back there soon or risk Ivar's wrath, yet at every step he felt himself on the verge of a discovery that would prove his prowess as an explorer. There was something in the air, something in the trembling of the leaves and the faint stirring of the wind that spoke to him. The deer had moved ahead of him, not randomly, it seemed, but with a sense of direction. Where was the animal leading him?

Now the land rose steeply, the trees thinned out, and a rocky escarpment loomed before him. It was rough land, but overgrown with bushes where berries might soon be ripening, and pocketed with tiny caves stuffed with leaves left over from the previous fall. Surely none of these could be the dark cave of his dreams?

There was no sign of the deer, and Rigg realized he had come to a turning point. Anxious to get back to his post, yet driven by the need to go one more stage and see what was beyond the escarpment, he decided to climb straight up rather than to search for the path where the deer must have disappeared.

Rigg shoved his axe in his belt, took a deep breath, and began to scramble up the bush-mottled side of the cliff. It was not a hard climb, but he tried to do it quietly without dislodging the stones or branches that surrounded him and keeping meanwhile an eye on the trail behind from which vantage point he would be easily seen by an enemy.

The idea of a bear in one of the deeper caves, the possibility of meeting some fearful snake—such real fears kept him moving fast, spurred him to cover each foot of the cliff with an upward sliding motion that was both agile and effective.

When he neared the top, he climbed more slowly, breathing heavily, resolving now to be cautious. He wanted to take stock of things, to have a good look around before he stood up in clear visibility at the summit sheering off a few feet above his head.

"I must go back soon," he said aloud, his own voice sounding strange, almost frightening in this lonely place.

With a final shove he reached the summit. There, clasping a sturdy root and crouching low against the rock, he peered over the edge of the escarpment. A small clearing interrupted the line of the forest trees, which stretched to a much greater height beyond. The sunlight blazed down, illuminating the grassy, stony patches of the glade and revealing in the centre the colossal wreck of a huge maple tree that had been split in two, probably by lightning. The two parts of the tree, half embedded in the rough soil, made a tangled barrier, a thicket of leaves and crisscrossing branches that caused Rigg to think at once of a shattered ship.

There was no sign of the deer, but as the boy's gaze steadied and fixed on the dark hollow of the tangled branches, he saw something move and rise in the shadows. For one awful moment Rigg caught his breath and clung fast to the rock. Then, with pounding heart, gasping yet trying hard not to scream, he swung down, scrambled, slipped, half fell, but somehow, within a few frantic minutes, found himself at the bottom of the escarpment.

There the panic returned, for staring at the wall of impenetrable bush, he was unsure at first of the way back.

*Only the fool acts without forethought,* Leif had

taught him, and Rigg closed his eyes, took three breaths, and looked again. The silence behind him, the obvious lack of pursuit, the feel of his axe in his hand—all these reassured him a little.

Finally he saw the place. A few broken twigs marked his path through the tangled branches. He dived into the bush—anything to get out of sight of that cliff. Racing along the path, he tried not to think of the fallen maple, of what he had seen in the clearing.

Rigg's return through those woods remained forever a blurred memory in his mind. The trees flew past, the bushes disappeared behind him. He leaped over small logs and dodged past thickets of brambles. He saw with joy the stone markers the Vikings had set up to point the trail: now he was at the edge of the forest.

A bare hillock rose before him. The sky seemed wider here, its blazing blue restoring his confidence. He ran on open ground and imagined he could smell the sea.

The crude timbers of the guard post loomed on the hill above. He would have to blow the horn, to give the warning. It was his duty. He would tell them all about the danger.

Ivar, the chieftain, his face twisted with anger, seemed to rise out of the hill just above him. Helgi and big Thrand, two of the best Viking swordsmen, crouched beside the post. Behind the men Rigg could see the home camp, the inlet, and the wide, open waters of the fjord. But the Viking horn, strung on one of the beams by a leather thong, seemed like an accusation.

Ivar looked the boy up and down, then remarked scornfully, "So, you've been exploring, have you? Asleep in the woods perhaps? Leaving your post and your duty behind. And you look very frightened. Did a bear chase you back here, or a bad dream?"

He took the boy by the shoulders and held him at arm's length. But Rigg shook free, seized the Viking horn, put it to his lips, and blew the alarm.

# ᛏᚺᛖ ᛒᛁᚻᛖᚠᚢᛁᚱᛁᚺ ᚾᛁᛰᚴ
# The Beleaguered Camp

Ivar and his men stood astonished. Then the chieftain grabbed the horn from Rigg's hand, yanking it clean from the stone and breaking the thong. He looked at it as if it were an evil thing and tossed it into the grass.

"What are you doing, boy? You mustn't give the warning without reason!" He grabbed Rigg by the shoulders and began to shake him as if he were a puppy or a newborn calf.

"But, Ivar..."

Down at the camp, a clamour of voices sounded. Figures ran frantically in and out of the main booth. Ivar let go of Rigg and gestured to one of his men. "Thrand, go at once and explain things. Tell them there is no attack. It's just the boy's foolishness."

"Ivar! It's not! There was something..."

All three Vikings looked at Rigg. Thrand made no move to go on his errand. The hubbub at the camp grew louder.

Ivar gestured to Thrand. "Go before everything collapses!"

As Thrand ran off toward the shore, Ivar wiped his sweating forehead with his sleeve. He glanced down the hill where Rigg had appeared from the woods, then gestured for the boy to sit on a boulder.

Ivar and Helgi stood over him and Ivar asked quietly, "Now think, boy, what did you see? You had a bad dream, isn't it so? You fell asleep in the woods and had a bad dream."

Rigg swallowed hard. He did not want to remember. Did he doubt his own senses? No, he had seen *the thing*. But how to explain it? They would never believe him—never.

Ivar bent closer and said hoarsely, "Speak, boy, or I'll outlaw you from the camp. I don't care what Leif thinks. You can live in the woods for all I care!"

Rigg caught his breath. Being made an outlaw was a terrible punishment to the Vikings. It took away all protection for the victim. It was bad enough in Greenland or Iceland, but here, in this unknown world, it was unthinkable.

Rigg bowed his head. "I...I saw a thing in the woods. I wasn't asleep. I tracked a deer up to a high place. There was a fallen tree. Something stood up as I watched."

"What do you mean, boy?" Ivar rasped. *"Something...?"*

Rigg looked first at Ivar, then at Helgi. He could see fear in the men's eyes. This was an empty land, that was the terror of it. But *something*?

"It was a demon," Rigg blurted out. The vision came back to him, and he felt his body tremble. He could not keep his hands still. "A demon in the shape of a man, but with a red face like a grinning mask. He stood up and looked at me. He started after me. He had some kind of weapon—I don't know!"

Ivar peered down at Rigg, then exchanged a look with Helgi. The chief began to laugh and Helgi with him. But Rigg sensed doubt and fear behind the laughter.

"No, no...it was a dream," Ivar said. "I know you're

given to such things. It's old Tyrkir with his runes and his magic. It's that witch Fianna, your mother. Long ago I warned Leif about her! Now confess, boy. It was a dream. You fell asleep and saw this in your mind."

Rigg, who had let the feared vision come back with force, could hardly speak. He shook his head and fought hard to keep control. "No, no..."

Ivar stared at him, his face twisted in an angry frown, his fists closing and unclosing in obvious frustration. Suddenly he gestured to Helgi, and the two men retreated out of Rigg's hearing. They stood on the other side of the large boulder and whispered for a while to each other.

Rigg got up, saw the Viking horn lying in the grass where Ivar had tossed it, and quickly picked it up. He reattached it to the thong on the wooden post. As Ivar and Helgi approached him, he remembered that Leif would hear of this, Leif would judge him. This thought inspired him to find the right words at last and he told the others, "Heimdall would not give a false warning, nor would I. You know that god will sound the call at the end of time. He will blow his horn when the world trembles, when Loki breaks free and the Midgard serpent rises in the waters. He will summon Thor and Odin and the other gods to battle. This poor horn is not Gjall, it is not Heimdall's horn, but I would not blow a false note any more than he!"

Ivar and Helgi stopped in their tracks and looked at him. The chief seemed to ponder this, then said, "Eloquent words, but we have already decided you will be removed from guard duty until further notice. I order you to take counsel with Tyrkir. He is an old dodderer and he sees too many things, but he wouldn't lie to me. He wouldn't endanger Leif's camp. Tyrkir will decide what you have seen or not seen and will tell us what to do. Meanwhile we will double the watch. Tomorrow I will take some men into the woods and search the place you describe. But you will remain in camp and talk to Tyrkir. That is my decision."

Rigg bowed his head. If he were older, he might have disputed this judgement with Ivar, but under the circumstances he could not. Besides, he needed desperately to talk to Tyrkir—and to his mother. He left Ivar and Helgi and, without once looking back, descended the long, gentle slope toward the shore of the broad lagoon and the Viking encampment.

Everyone had approved Leif's choice of a landing place—a large, tranquil bay at the end of a vast fjord. Here a brook flowed from a quiet lagoon that was nearly closed on the bay side by a long bar of sand and gravel. Although they had encountered no living being and found no traces of any human settlement, although the great new lands appeared quite empty, the Vikings knew that on this spot they would be safe from surprise attack from either land or sea. Looking landward, in fact, they had a pleasant view of grassy fields and marshes, with the dark forests climbing the hills behind.

On this spot the original thirty-six voyagers had built their booths and some adjacent huts, their smelting pit, and their smithy. And the new *knarr*, the ship that would taken them home should Leif not reappear, was even now under construction on a site between the lagoon and the bay and fjord.

It was only after Leif's departure that the others had become uneasy and had hastened to build the new ship. Only then—perhaps because they missed Leif's ready humour and eternal optimism—did they begin to feel themselves isolated and vulnerable, poised precariously between a bleak, empty fjord on one side and an unknown, frightening forest on the other. The new ship, they knew, would take them away from any threat that might appear on the land side, precisely the direction they feared most.

Now Rigg, who had given first warning of such a threat, found himself reassured a little by the sight of the sunlit water, the Vikings' hulking booths, and the men going in and out about their business. A few, having heard the alarm, eyed him curiously as he approached. Thrand, who had come down to quiet the camp, and at that moment stood talking to two of the Vikings beside the smithy, gave Rigg a scornful look. Undaunted, the boy threw back his shoulders and walked proudly by.

He knew he had sounded the alarm for good reason. The figure in his dream had come to life and had risen like a terrible spectre from the dark forest. Despite what Ivar and the others believed or pretended, and despite his anger and humiliation at being removed from the guard post, Rigg was certain he had encountered a being who posed a real threat to the encampment. It was not merely a dream. As he recalled the event, the boy shuddered, certain he had met a hostile supernatural power, for like the rest of the Vikings, Rigg believed that supernatural beings were as real as any stone or tree and that they had the power to hurt human flesh. Ivar, for all his talk of dreams, feared such power. His idea that Rigg must consult Tyrkir was evidence that, despite his scornful words, he half believed what Rigg had told him. And only Tyrkir, with his experience of weird things, would know what to do if indeed the Vikings had to face a new and terrible fact: that they were by no means alone in this vast and terrifying land.

# ᚾᛁᛏᛏᛁᚾ ᛏ�æᛏ ᚱᚢᚾᛁᛋ
# Casting the Runes

Fianna, Rigg's mother, a tall sharp-eyed youngish woman whose red hair was already streaked with grey, appeared at the door of the main booth. She wore a long plain yellow dress and leather sandals. Like all Viking women, she also wore a brooch to which some handy domestic items—knife, scissors, needle, and thread—were attached by thin chains. As she put her arm around Rigg, these metal objects tinkled familiarly.

Quickly Fianna drew her son into a large chamber, one that smelled of smoke and old animal grease. It was the main kitchen and meeting room and a fire burned there constantly. One or two men dozed on benches by the wall.

This was the central room of the main building. On one side were the chief's sleeping quarters, on the other a few smaller compartments, one of which was occupied by Rigg, his mother, and Tyrkir, all of whom had high standing because of their connections with Leif.

Rigg's mother had been taken as a slave in Ireland and had been freed by Leif from her thralldom, as had Tyrkir, the German. The boy's relationship with them

18

caused a few of the Vikings, including Ivar, to be skeptical about his worth, but most of the men were quite tolerant. Although slaves were of lesser social status, they were considered fully human by the Vikings and when freed often enjoyed a special status, especially if they had unique skills, powers, or patrons.

Tyrkir himself was a rune caster and a wizard. He had learned his craft among the Druids in the German forests and then in the great city the Vikings called Miklagard, and which some knew as Byzantium or Constantinople. As they entered the small sleeping room, Rigg was not surprised to see the old man already sitting with his familiar bag of magic stones—runes carved on small pieces of antler bone—on which one could read fate and the future. Obviously he and Fianna had already divined that Rigg needed their help.

A large candle flickered, casting shadows on the walls and on Tyrkir's hooded face. Without a word Rigg sat beside him. Fianna, too, seated herself, her blue eyes regarding her son with affection. Tyrkir gazed at the boy as if he were looking straight through him, but said nothing. He had assumed his black wizard's robe, a garment on which an eerie pattern of small blue human eyes had been embroidered. This pattern alluded to the god Odin's sacrifice in giving up one of his eyes to learn the secret of casting the runes.

"You sounded the alarm," Rigg's mother said. "Thrand told us it was a false signal."

"It wasn't," Rigg said firmly. He felt Tyrkir's dark glance on him. His mother reached out and pressed his hand. "It was the dream that started it," he continued. "You remember the dream of the deer, but it wasn't a dream in the end. I saw...something. It was—"

Rigg began to describe his encounter. Tyrkir bent over, listening. His mother gasped as he reached the terrifying climax.

There was a silence, then finally Tyrkir spoke. His

voice was deep but also hoarse, an old man's voice, his words oddly inflected. "When reality mirrors a dream, it is time to take notice. I will have some words with Ivar."

"And he'll listen," Rigg said eagerly. "He's frightened by all this. Tomorrow he will search the woods, but he wants your opinion, too. He wants to know what we're dealing with."

"So do I," Tykir answered. He held out the bag of runes. "Now close your eyes, son, and compose your mind. Think back to what you saw in the forest, and when you are ready, choose the rune."

Rigg shuddered a little as he began to meditate. He knew the rune he chose would determine much in the next days. He fixed his mind on the scene in the forest, and as he did so his hands trembled a little. When they stopped shaking, he reached into the bag, drew out a rune, and placed it on the small table Tyrkir had drawn up between them for that purpose.

Tyrkir looked at the rune and nodded gravely. It was a simple figure taking the shape almost of the letter *H*.

"*Hagalaz,*" the old man named it. "Right side up, upside down—it makes no difference. It is the rune of disruption. Everything is going to change. Something new and powerful will enter our lives."

There was a moment of silence, then Fianna murmured, "The figure in the forest—was it a magical being then?"

Tyrkir shrugged. "It is too early to tell. What the rune says is that we cannot sit here and build our boat and wait for Leif's return. We must take action, or events will overwhelm us. The secret of everything lies in the forest. You tell us, Rigg, that Ivar plans to search the forest in the morning. I predict that Ivar will not go very far into those woods and that he will find nothing. Which means that we will be at the mercy of whatever lurks out there. No, there is a great need for some real action, and I fear, Rigg, that you and I must be the ones to undertake it. We must go into the forest and discover whatever is hiding there."

Rigg could not believe his ears. Go into the forest with Tyrkir? The very thought made his heart beat faster. But then he remembered—Ivar would never allow it. And his mother?

"Tyrkir, I've been confined to the shore," he said. "Ivar won't let me go."

The old man shook his head. "Ivar is a fool. A brave fool, but a fool nonetheless. If we do not go to meet what is out there, it will come to us on its own terms. I do not think we will like those terms."

Fianna stood and began to pace the small chamber. "Tyrkir, sometimes I think you're a fool yourself. A boy and an old man alone in that forest? You can't be serious! If you go, we'll never see you again. I don't want to lose my only son to this hateful land!"

Tyrkir got to his feet slowly. He thrust his hood back, his scraggly silver hair shining in the candlelight, his face wearing a sly smile. He had great respect for Fianna, but he always relished seeing her in a temper. Rigg swallowed the protest he was about to make to Fianna. It would sound ridiculous to press the point on his mother—that he was old enough to scout in the woods. She knew very well he was old enough, and skilled enough. Clearly, though, she was worried about what they might find there. It was up to Tyrkir to reassure her about that.

But Fianna faced them and spoke first. "In the old country—I mean, Ireland and not bare Greenland—I used to listen to my grandfather's stories. He told me what he'd heard from his own grandfather, that our people long ago crossed the water and found new lands. Whether great islands or even larger places like this one, no one knows. Leif is the first Viking to step on land here, but the day he did so I told him that my people had been here before him. Being Leif he only laughed and said, 'What? In those cockleshells?' Leif never thought much of the Irish boats. Still, I believe the stories. The Irish—St.

Brendan for one—came over to this land of demons long before the Vikings, and even he wasn't the first."

"Who was the first, Mother?" Rigg asked. He had heard some of this before, but every time his mother spoke she added something, and he was eager to learn the whole story.

"No one knows, although some say races of giants, or troglodytes, or the demons that consorted with Lilith in the desert, or the lost tribes of Israel. God only knows what you saw in the forest, or why this old man wants to take you back there to look again!"

Tyrkir no longer tried to conceal his amusement. He smiled broadly, showing his strong white teeth, then shook his head, as if in resignation, and took Fianna's hand. "I have travelled far, once to the eastern lands, to the place they call Rus, as far as any Viking raider, and everywhere I expected to find strange beings I found only men."

"Are you saying there are *men* in that forest?" Fianna questioned him. It was clear she thought the idea ridiculous.

"I was born in a country of great forests. I find nothing strange in men living in such places."

"But this was no man," Rigg insisted. "This was a red demon from a nightmare! I'm not afraid of him, though. If the rune says I must go back and deal with him, I will."

"There is no shame in fear," Tyrkir told him, "and no virtue in bravado. We must move wisely and take all precautions. For all I know there may be men here so wild that they are hardly human. Or some ancient folk may have consorted with demons, or with the children of Cain, and been banished here. There may be troll or dwarf races somewhere, as the Viking stories tell, and perhaps close by us here. Or you may have stumbled on a mound inhabited by one of the *huldufolk*, the hidden people. You and I, Rigg, do not want to be captured and locked forever in one of these mountains, do we? We do not want to meet any wild Irish folk left behind by St. Brendan..." He winked at Fianna, laughed, and continued. "I joke, but only to cheer our spirits. We are confronted by a mystery, and the rune tells us to deal with it. It does not tell us we will be successful."

Fianna pressed the old man's hands tightly in hers. "Must you take my son?"

"When will he learn to be a man, if not now?"

Rigg started to speak, but then he noticed that two Vikings had stepped into the small chamber. One of them was Thrand, the burly guard and friend of Ivar. He seemed, however, to have suddenly lost all his arrogance and bluster. Although his sword was drawn, he clasped it with a white-knuckled fist and his face was pale and frozen. His companion, a good man nicknamed the Owl because he preferred the night watches, looked equally pale and shaken.

When they mumbled and pointed without getting any words out, Tyrkir barked at them impatiently, "What is it? Some trouble, I see! If you cannot say it, then show us. Lead the way quickly, men, so we can deal with it."

The two Vikings turned and hastened out. Rigg followed with the others through the central chamber, now deserted, and out into the broad yard between the Viking booths. A small group of men stood there, heads tilted as if dazed, looking at nothing.

"What is it?" Rigg cried out.

The hills, the great lagoon, the distant forests—everything looked peaceful and unchanged.

Thrand put one finger to his lips. "Listen!"

Then Rigg heard it—a low, steady drumming, maddening in its monotony and menacing in its alien purpose, sounding from the forest beyond the camp.

The Vikings looked helplessly at one another, then at the old man.

"*Hagalaz,*" Tyrkir muttered, spitting on the ground.

# An Evil Beginning

Ivar came down the hill toward the camp. He walked quickly, his broad shoulders slumping a little, his long fingers playing nervously across the hilt of his sword. Once or twice he looked back at the forest, and from time to time he shook his head as if he wanted to get the incessant drumming out of his ears.

All the Vikings seemed to feel the same way. In Greenland, when the Norse settled, there had been no native peoples, and this bush drumming was quite alien to them. Even Rigg, who was excited by this new development, soon found that the drums irritated him and made him edgy. Tyrkir, for his part, looked very grave.

Rolf, the Viking navigator, a stocky fellow with a bald head and shining blue eyes, now addressed the rune master. "Old man, you've been to many countries. What in Thor's name can this racket be?"

"Be careful! Do not listen too closely," Tyrkir warned. "It may be an enchantment. I have heard an old tale about a sailor who had to make passage of some rocky islets where the songs of spirit women came near to destroying him." The rune master wore a sly smile that might have been meant to cheer them up.

"How did he prevent it?" Thrand asked.

"He put wax in his ears."

"He was a coward then," sneered Ivar, who strode up at that moment to join them. He eyed them all fiercely, drew himself up to his full height, and tapped his sword lightly. "Are we men and warriors or old women? Even Helgi, whom I took to be a fighter, went pale when I asked him to keep watch up there."

Ivar rubbed his dark beard with his fist and started to draw figures in the sand with his sword point. "I'll take six men and this whelp of a boy as our guide. Tyrkir will come, too, to interpret the signs. We won't wait until morning. We'll go immediately without eating dinner. Who knows what will happen when darkness falls? We must deal with this menace right now. Some will guard the camp, the rest of us will attack. That is my decision."

"But, Ivar," Thrand protested, "suppose it is a spirit or a demon? The boy told us—" Here the warrior stopped, wiped his sweating brow, and shrugged.

The chief's ferocious eye held him silent. "You can stay behind and sweep the booth if you wish, Thrand. But I took you for more of a man than that."

The Viking, stung to a fury, moved his hand toward his sword, then thought better of it. He stared at his feet and said no more.

Rigg could see that Ivar was full of fear, but that he was fighting it by attempting to be strong, by making plans and building up his own confidence. He was try-ing to get a grip on himself, and the boy admired that. Still, the fact that their chief was afraid was unsettling.

"Here's the plan," Ivar told them, and Rigg drew close to the men's circle. "The boy will lead us to the hill where he saw the demon. We will approach from two sides. Tyrkir will try to destroy the enemy with his magic battle spells. If that fails, I will become *hamrammr*—I will change into a bear and destroy the thing."

A murmur of awed approval went around the circle of men, and Rigg felt a thrill of excitement. He had heard that Ivar had the power of shape-shifting, that in certain circumstances he could change into the likeness of a ferocious animal, a bear or a wolf, and attack without mercy, impervious to pain or to the enemy's weapons. All the Vikings believed this was possible; some claimed to have seen it with their own eyes.

"Thrand," Ivar ordered, "you fetch my bearskin and the lucky amulet. The rest of you get ready. We will not sleep tonight with those taunting drums in our ears." He strode away toward the main booth, and the men began to move in all directions. Some went to gather their weapons, others to see to their camp duties. It was still light, but a slight chill indicated the coming of evening.

Fianna drew her son aside. "If Ivar goes berserk, you must stay out of his way. He dislikes you, and when a man is berserk, he may do anything or attack anyone. Stay close to Tyrkir. He is the only one who can protect you."

Rigg nodded and followed his mother back to the sleeping room. Tyrkir was already changing clothes, casting off his gown for a leather jerkin and a long blue cloak. Rigg took down the bow given him by Leif and collected some arrows. He strapped on a short sword and put on a leather helmet. He did not bother with armour. It occurred to him that speed might be more useful in the coming struggle than protective wrappings.

When both men had clothed themselves to their satisfaction, Rigg spoke his thoughts to Tyrkir. "Perhaps our expedition won't be necessary now. Perhaps the problem will be solved tonight and we'll find and destroy our enemy."

Tyrkir looked at the boy. "Have you not observed the

forests out there, spread across the whole country, the millions of leaves on those trees? The leaves, although countless, are fewer by far than the possibilities we may face in this new land. I do not believe that nine or ten of us can resolve anything with a few swords and axes. Later I will tell Ivar about the rune you drew, about the meaning of *Hagalaz*, a rune that cannot be solved so simply. It is a very complicated thing, a very big disruption that the rune predicts. I think we will need a longer and more complete exploration. Yes, you and I will still go. But I did not want to tell Ivar that."

"Why?" Rigg asked.

"Because he was working himself out of his panic and into a state of courage and I did not want to discourage him."

"Be sure you watch over my son," Fianna said. "And think carefully about what you see out there. I don't like the sound of those drums. It means the danger is greater than even you imagined, rune master. You yourself said the drums may be an enchantment."

"Yes, I said that, Fianna, but perhaps I spoke too quickly. A second thought occurs to me, one that is even more frightening than my first notion."

"And what is that?" she asked.

"That the drums, far from being an enchantment, may be a signal. That some being, some enemy out there, is communicating something."

"Communicating something?" Rigg wondered aloud at this. "But what is the message? And who is listening?"

"We are," Tyrkir said with a harsh laugh. "Whatever being is out there has got our attention and is now moving us into its field of power. Now farewell, Fianna. Have no fear. I will bring your son back."

"I will bring myself back," Rigg said, and marched straight out of the room, not even stopping to embrace his mother.

Outside, the two of them found the Viking exploring

party already clad in armour and bearing spears, axes, and bows and arrows. Besides Ivar and Thrand, the Owl had been chosen to join them, also Silk Beard, the Crow, Ragnar, Ulf, and Hedin, good men all, skilled with weapons and experienced in battle.

Thrand carried a small leather satchel. Rigg knew it contained the berserker's magic amulet and the bearskin he would put on when he transformed himself. It would take Ivar only a few seconds to assume the skin, but much longer to go *hamslauss*, to twist himself out of human shape and to take on the form of a magic animal. This process would be accelerated, Rigg decided, just because Ivar was already so jumpy: you could imagine him within minutes sliding right out of his senses and into his wild animal nature.

"The berserker is in all of us," Leif had once told his son. "It's just a question of when it will come out."

Which was an odd thing for Leif to say. Rigg remembered thinking that Leif was the least edgy person he had ever met. A more sensible, humorous, and earthbound man the boy had never heard of. But how would Leif have faced these drums, how would he have kept his composure in the face of their incessant beating?

The boy trudged up the hill, following the little band of warriors who had already placed themselves in attack readiness. As they marched up to the guard post, Rigg turned only once to wave to Fianna, who stood at the entrance of the main booth. She did not wave back but made a sign in the air, some magic gesture perhaps, although not the sign of the cross.

These Westvikings were still pagans to the core, and Fianna, who had been brought up as a Christian, had eagerly accepted their ways. She was a natural-born witch, she said, one the Christian monks would probably have burned at the stake. Among the Vikings she was able to put all her woman's lore into practice, and to use rituals and skills taught to her by her grandmother after the old customs.

As the drums pounded steadily around them, the sound seeming to rise from the trembling earth itself, Rigg murmured a spell, using the old Celtic words taught him long ago by his mother: *"Off and away! All evil things depart. The gods keep us well in body, in good heart."*

When they approached the top of the hill, Ivar spoke to Silk Beard, telling him to take over Helgi's watch.

"If you wish," Silk Beard replied, running his fingers through his silvery whiskers in characteristic fashion. "But I would rather be fighting beside you in the forest."

Ivar frowned. "I know—but what's that lazy good-for-nothing Helgi up to? He's gone to sleep on his watch! And with the drums sounding everywhere like Ragnarok itself, like the end of the world."

As the warriors reached the crest of the hill, they saw the wooden stake, with the Viking horn attached, jutting up, and the smooth, round boulder just beside it. Helgi, half concealed by the boulder, lay facing the deep forest. He appeared to have fallen asleep.

A couple of the Vikings laughed. "He's fighting battles in his dreams," someone jeered.

"The drums have put him in a trance," the Owl guessed.

Tyrkir, however, who had walked around in front of the recumbent man, stopped suddenly, his gaze fixed on Helgi. The rune master seemed to be studying Helgi's posture and also his face, which the others could not see clearly. Then Tyrkir closed his eyes and murmured something incomprehensible.

Rigg ran over to get a better view. He, too, froze. Helgi's face, most often full of colour, ruddy, and healthy, was now a dire white. His eyes, round and staring, gazed sightlessly at the wilderness beyond. His hands were clenched helplessly together. He had not drawn his weapon.

"He is dead," Tyrkir told them. "Helgi is dead."

Ivar came forward and gave the rune master an incredulous look. Then he bent over and shook Helgi's body, once, twice, before he turned away in horror and helplessness. "No mark on him," he whispered, "no sign of any struggle. Poor Helgi's been killed by a spell. The demons out there, in those woods, have killed him!"

The Vikings erupted in anger and muttered threats. They stirred, shook their weapons, but seemed helpless to act.

The drums continued to sound from the forest.

Then Tyrkir, who had bent once again over the body, got slowly to his feet. "No spell killed Helgi, I will warrant. At least not the kind you might imagine. Look at him, look at the poor man's features, at the colour of his face and the way his hands and his body are contorted. No, Helgi did not die of any spell. He died of fright. Something came out of the woods and scared him to death."

Ivar gaped at the rune master, as if only half taking in his words. The chieftain walked a few paces away from the group and stared for some time at the deep woods. Then he raised his head and gave a loud, soul-chilling cry. It was an inarticulate singing speech, yet it resembled the howl of wolf. At the same time it was far more unnatural, far stranger, just because it was neither human nor animal.

Thrand, his big hands shaking, walked toward their chief, holding out the pouch containing the bearskin.

# The Broken Circle

Tyrkir stepped in front of Thrand. The red-faced, burly Viking glared at him, but did not challenge the rune master. Tyrkir turned to their chieftain, who had fallen on all fours and was scratching at the earth, shaking and trembling, as if he were trying to wriggle out of his own skin.

"Ivar, no! Listen, the drums have stopped." Tyrkir's words made them all pause to listen. "We must take other action now."

Ivar gazed up at him with the half-comprehension of a drunken man. His howling and groaning had ceased. He seemed to be emerging from some terrible vision, from the coils of a nightmare. When he stood, he looked unsteady. His hands trembled and his eyes refused to focus. Yet he was clearly coming back to himself. He cocked his head to listen, seemed satisfied that the drums were not beating, and when Tyrkir bade him sit on the boulder to rest, he did so.

Rigg, too, was relieved. Uneasily he waited with the others for a resumption of the ominous signal, but none came.

31

A wonderful silence enveloped everything. The trees stirred in the gentlest of winds, the bushes and low grass wore a ruffled look, in the distance the waves sounded—nothing otherwise disturbed the peace of the lengthening afternoon. Rigg had not realized how the incessant drumming had affected him and the others, how the alien rhythms had bent their minds out of shape and unbalanced their judgements.

Now Tyrkir moved to take charge. "Thrand, be sensible. There is no one for Ivar to challenge. We must make our plans quickly. We must see to poor Helgi. The enemy has given us some respite, and we must take advantage of it."

Thrand, clearly unhappy with Tyrkir's boldness, answered with a sneer, then said, "Who appointed you our leader, old man? It wasn't Leif, as I recall. I take no orders from foreign thralls. I await the command of Ivar, who will decide what action we take next."

There was a murmur of approval from some of the other Vikings, but Ivar growled and waved his arm. He swung his sword gingerly, clasping it with one hand while he rubbed his cheeks and beard with the other. His clear eyes told them he was back in full possession of his senses. "Never mind...have no fear, men. You'll see who is leader when the battle comes. Let's listen to what the old man has in mind. We can't waste a moment, but I warn you, Tyrkir, I'm not going back to the booths like a defeated man. We must avenge the death of Helgi. Whoever was responsible must die."

"*If* anyone was responsible, Ivar," Tyrkir said. "We do not know for sure how he died. That is what I would like to find out. And I propose to do so. We do not need warriors yet. Rigg and I can go into the forest and find out who our enemies are. That was the plan I had already thought of even before Helgi's death. It has some advantages. The boy and I will be more invisible than a troop of fighting men. I can read the signs and interpret things and the boy is fleet of foot and wily. If I am snared, he can escape and bring the news. It is better that you give Helgi a funeral, set up a strong guard here, and await our return. When we bring back the news, you will know what to do."

There was a moment of silence as Ivar and the others contemplated this. Then the Owl asked, "What if you don't come back?"

Ivar raised his hand for silence. He sheathed his sword and walked among the men, slapping one or two on the shoulder, looking them in the eyes and only stopping abruptly before Helgi's lifeless body. "That's exactly what I fear. That you may not come back. And here's my decision. We'll give you five days to return. If you fail to appear, we won't seek you out. We'll work more speedily to complete the *knarr*, load her with as much cargo as possible, and sail as soon as we can. This is a country for spirits and wizards and not for men. It is a place of riddles. I long for a good old-fashioned raid and some priest's silver in my long ship. This forest is not to my liking, and I can't avenge Helgi against the ghouls."

At this the men murmured their approval. Ragnar, Ulf, and a couple of others were already swinging up the body of the dead man to carry him back to the camp.

"Two men on guard here from now on," Ivar commanded, "and we'll double the other guards, too."

"But, Tyrkir, when will we go?" Rigg asked, gazing from the shoreline and booths to the forest beyond them.

"At once. Let us travel as far as we can before dark." He was already striding down the hill toward the forest.

Rigg made a few hasty farewells and ran to catch up to him.

"Good luck, rune master!" Ivar shouted. "If I'm not mistaken, you'll need it."

The rune master and the boy walked boldly into the deep woods, making their way along the almost invisible trail Rigg had fled down only hours before. It was getting late, though here and there sunlight still pierced the thick canopy of leaves. They moved through a tangle of underbrush, green storied branches above them, old logs, damp leaf and moss underfoot. They climbed over strewn boulders, tramped warily across the rare clearings, and crossed one or two tiny rain-washed gullies. The leaves rustled lightly, birds sang, insects darted and buzzed.

Giant maples and hundred-foot-high yellow birches surrounded them, or evergreens opened dim alleys where they trod, it seemed, on padded feet. Squirrels darted here and there, a blue jay sang on the boughs of a wild cherry tree; they could smell a skunk and something rank and fierce, perhaps a bear.

After a while they seemed divorced from human life and contact, remote, insignificant, and vulnerable. Rigg had not the slightest idea which tree he had climbed and where he had seen the deer, so changed was everything in the early evening's angled light. Yet he knew this must be the right way, and once or twice, when Tyrkir glanced inquiringly at him, he nodded confidently and plunged forward.

Time passed and the undergrowth thinned out, the land began to rise, and the familiar rocky cliffs appeared above the dark line of the treetops. For the first time in their relentless, silent trek Rigg knew exactly where he was. The breeze stirred and he shivered. He stopped and looked questioningly at the rune master.

Had he really run so far in flight from the thing on the plateau?

Tyrkir, however, was preoccupied. The old man had bent over some bushes that grew beside an animal track, only to come up with a handful of small blood-coloured berries. He sampled a few, then offered some to Rigg.

"Raspberries," the rune master mused. "I remember when Leif landed, how I got lost and kept alive eating berries and hazelnuts. When they found me, I showed him all the berry bushes and he got the idea to call this country Vinland. 'Grapes will be more appealing than berries,' your father told me. 'And when people make the voyage, they won't find them and will be puzzled, and I will meanwhile take all the timber and furs that I can find here!' Leif always had a sense of humour," the rune master concluded. He laughed and wiped his hands on the grass. "So that is the place up there, is it?"

Rigg nodded.

"Well, I think I can climb that cliff, but I hope there is none higher," the rune master said. "I do not think whatever it was you saw will be up there still, but we are not alone in these woods—I can feel it. And that bothers me."

"You, too?" On their walk Rigg had half suppressed the strong sense that they were being observed and possibly followed, but he could not imagine a human moving so quietly beside them. Perhaps there were strange spirits in these woods. Well, it was too late to worry about that now!

They climbed, Rigg leading the way and feeling exposed on the open cliff face with the full sunlight bearing down on his back. Tyrkir had more trouble with the ascent than he had anticipated. Once or twice he paused for breath, his frail body heaving with exhaustion and effort, his bony hands clutching at the rocks and tree roots.

"Oh, for a magic carpet such as they tell of in the East," he moaned. But he hung on and slowly joined Rigg near the rim of the precipice.

Together they peered over a huge rock slab and saw the great lightning-struck tree where Rigg had sighted the demon figure.

"Remember poor Helgi, struck dead by something he could not fathom," Tyrkir said. "We must be strong in ourselves. We must find an inner power of resistance. Do not imagine more than you see, and test what you see against your mind's eye. Now, since this great clearing appears to be empty—except for that moose standing still against the forest yonder—we can go cautiously forward."

Despite his keen eyes, Rigg had not seen the moose. He must do as the rune master advised and use his senses better. He stood and walked along with Tyrkir. They proceeded slowly, since there was no possibility of concealment.

As they approached, the great fallen maple loomed like a daunting wall of wood. Its slashed trunk, split branches, and scraggly bush might have been the work of Thor's hammer itself. The dark hollow where the red thing had arisen to startle Rigg seemed empty now of all but shadow.

"But see, there is smooth earth, cleared earth perhaps, right where the trunk divides!" Tyrkir pointed and Rigg saw the place. It was an open patch of earth set with small objects, a ten-foot-square piece of land on which small white objects had been set in rows and circles. This did not look like nature's work. They drew closer, and the sun glinted off the objects—stones or shells or bones?

"An animal picked clean by scavengers?" Tyrkir wondered aloud. "No...it cannot be. I see it now!" He stopped and held Rigg's arm tightly. "Keep calm," he warned. "Stay very calm. I see it is a human skull. Perhaps the figure you encountered here emanated from that. Is this the haunt of a *gast* or a *svipa*, of an old spirit trapped in the objects there? Was that what flared out when you came before? We must be very careful. There is magic here, but of what kind I am not sure."

Although his heart was pounding wildly, Rigg was determined to stay calm, but then something happened. A grey-black shape bolted suddenly from beneath the hollow trunk, flashed across their field of vision, and disappeared.

Startled, Rigg stumbled forward into the cleared space. He tripped and sprawled full-length, his body slamming down on some of the objects set there. The skull, bleached white and ominous, rolled in ghastly movement away from his fingertips. A little row of balanced bones, arranged, it seemed, as pointers, tottered and fell beside him where he lay.

Tyrkir gasped and came up beside the boy. He stood expectantly, as if waiting for something to happen, then, when nothing did, he began to chastise the sheepish Rigg, reaching down at the same time to help the embarrassed boy to his feet.

"Now you have done it!" the old man muttered, brushing him off and touching the boy's cheek lightly with an accusing finger. "You have broken the magic pattern. Who knows what we are in for now?"

Rigg started to apologize, but Tyrkir continued, his gimlet glance fixing the boy. "Do you not remember that rune you turned up? *Hagalaz*—disruption. And now we are part of that. We have upset things by coming here. Just look around you! Those bones must be sacred objects, and these lines on the earth form a magic circle made by some being who lives here. Magic is always for a purpose. Someone, or *some thing*, I fear, will not be pleased. And who knows whether we can put things right?"

ᛏᚱᚱᚲ ᚺᛁᛁ ᛁᚺᚤᛁᚺᛏᛁᛁ ᚲᛁᛏᚫᛁ

# Dark and Nameless Paths

Rigg looked from the rune master, past the tangled boughs and dark upturned roots of the old tree, to the impassive forest wall that enclosed the clearing. The skull lay at his feet, staring up at him in empty-eyed indifference. The boy felt blind and helpless. How could he ever learn the secrets of a world where nothing was what it seemed, where unexpected dangers lurked behind every tree and bush? He half believed now that Ivar was right: the sooner the Vikings returned to a familiar land the better.

But Tyrkir, as if reading Rigg's thoughts, patted him reassuringly on the shoulder. "A groundhog runs out of its lair, a young man falls, and the circle is broken. But, Rigg, the circle was destined to be broken. Do not blame yourself. What could these bones mean—and who or what set them here—that is the question."

Rigg looked again. The skull had been carefully placed in the centre of the circle. The bones had been laid out to form a circle of their own within the larger circle. Worlds within worlds...

"Look here, footprints!" Tyrkir pointed to a few shallow marks in the sand. "Someone wearing sandals—a man, made these. The animals have not disturbed things. Why? Because everything was done so recently. What you saw here was a man and not a demon. Someone made this circle. He set the skull on this high, cleared space, facing the sea and our camp."

Rigg stared at the rune master. "You mean this was put here because of us?"

Tyrkir nodded. "It might be so. What does a circle mean? Protection! Whoever made this might want to keep us out."

"But why didn't they attack us?"

Tyrkir shrugged. "Perhaps they are not warriors. Perhaps we frightened them. They may be hunters who have come here for the first time. That is what we must find out."

"There are no demons then?"

"I did not say there were no demons. I said whoever made this must be a man."

For some time Tyrkir was silent. He bent over and carefully arranged the skull and bones in their original patterns. In one place, though, he left a break in the circle. There he scratched a rune sign on the hard earth. When he finished, he straightened and smiled at Rigg. "Now we will try to track our trackers. How good are you at reading bush signs?"

Rigg laughed. He had learned quite a lot in the season he had spent in this new world. Leif, the Owl, and sharp-eyed Ragnar had taught him. He knew he was the best of the Vikings at following a bush trail.

"I missed the footprints just now, though," he said quietly. "And I nearly lost my way when the demon—or man—appeared to me."

"You were distracted, surprised. But now you can point us along the proper trail. It is getting dark and we must go somewhat farther before we make our camp."

Rigg nodded and led the way around the thick, moss-grown trunk of the fallen tree. Behind it, in the low scrub, he found a few signs, faint tracks, bent grass and twigs, showing someone's recent passage.

They entered the forest again and beat their way upward through a stand of huge pines. Here the trail vanished in the softly carpeted undergrowth.

"I feel this is right, even though I see no marks," Rigg explained.

The rune master smiled and nodded. They went on steadily climbing until they came out on a ridge sheltered by poplars and large maples. Below lay a valley of seemingly impenetrable wilderness. To the west the hills rolled away in dark green waves, but gold and umber tints among the leaves hinted at the oncoming autumn. There was a chill in the air. The first stars had appeared in the cloudless gold-blue sky. They heard the soft rush of distant water, but could see no glint of a stream. Far to their left, to the southeast, the shore lay. It would be almost unreachable, but they knew it must be there, a fact that gave these seagoing Vikings some comfort.

They trekked on and Rigg found more signs—a few broken branches and the faint track of a sandal or shoe stamped across an anthill. Then they plunged into the bushland, working their way down through the deep woods. They no longer felt they were spied upon—perhaps they had imagined that part of it, or perhaps they had taken the bait and needed no further watching.

Yet nothing seemed to move in the bush, except a few small animals and birds, hare and squirrel and fox, an occasional brown bear, sighted at a distance, or blue jays and partridges, startled by the intruders. Once they saw a heron cruising away toward some marshy haven.

Another hour's trek and they found themselves immersed in the thickest part of the bush. By now, they reckoned, they must be at the bottom of the valley. Sure enough, the rushing water sounded closer here, and when they followed the sound, they came at last to the river itself, a pure, fast-running stream curving down from a glen and flashing between several large, moss-grown boulders.

"Here is our campsite," Tyrkir announced, but Rigg knew it already. He was pleased with the place—except for the damp chill that clung to it—and they settled in to build a small shelter beside the largest of the boulders, gathering balsam branches for the purpose and contriving a roof of sorts with moss and leaves and a few wooden stakes that they lashed together with wild vines.

When this work was finished, Rigg did a brief reconnoiter around the perimeter of the camp. At one point, close beside the stream, he found another circle—this time made of stones, set up for a small fire. The stones enclosed ashes. He poked at them and found them cold. Then he looked farther and found several footprints in the damp earth by the river.

Rigg pointed these out to Tyrkir, and the old man simply nodded. "Soon," he murmured, "soon now."

After that they built their own fire and feasted on some of the dried venison and salted whale meat they had brought along with them. They cooked wild greens and cabbage and finished off with blueberries smeared on flatbread.

When the darkness settled slowly, they covered themselves with balsam branches and lay down in their improvised shelter. Rigg stayed awake a long time, listening to the night noises. The twitter of birds sounded above the rushing stream, and he felt reassured, but when past midnight he heard noises nearly like these but subtly different, he wondered if indeed he heard birds— or signals meant to sound like bird song.

After that he tossed restlessly beside the old man. The chill of the night penetrated the shelter, and just when the first light appeared high above and far away through the willow branches that overhung the shelter, he fell deeply asleep.

He was awakened by blinding beams of light, the smell of smoke, and roasting meat. Tyrkir had gathered some mushrooms and was grilling them on a stick to go with the dried venison he had warmed up. "When we finish, I have something to show you," he said.

After breakfast they put out the fire, smoothed over the earth, threw the boughs and stakes away, and removed all obvious traces of their campsite.

"Look, we have found a real trail at last," Tyrkir said, pointing. As he spoke, he led Rigg across the shallows of the river and up the embankment on the other side. One of the birch trees there had been stripped of some bark. A splash of red marked the spot. Certainly it looked like a trail sign, but they could not be sure.

Their doubts were resolved, however, when they ventured a little farther, climbing up through a stand of maples and pausing beside two large boulders that might almost have been an ancient gateway. On the stone they noticed crude drawings, the shapes of antlered deer or moose perhaps, or of birds in full flight, a vivid red on the grey stone.

"Hunters," Tyrkir guessed. "They may have wandered into this region. Perhaps our presence has thrown them into confusion. In any case, they are cautious and possibly fearful."

"Are these the old people my mother spoke of—the ones who came from Ireland first to this country?"

"A red man rising from the ground to startle you. Red marks on the trees and stones. If these are the old settlers from your mother's country, then they have adopted strange ways in their sojourn here. We must approach them with caution. In the east I heard many tales of the *anthropophagi*, odd people who are only half human and who feast on human flesh. What does red signify but blood? I do not want to end up in a cannibal's stomach."

Rigg could not help but laugh. "You might be too indigestible, although if they know you're a wise man, they might cook you merely to taste your wisdom."

"I will pretend to be an idiot then. Now let us go cautiously up this trail."

They trekked on, stage by stage, resting when they had to in the bushes, not showing themselves except to examine the signs on the trees, of which there were several more examples. The country favoured them, for the thickness of the woods did not abate and there was plenty of cover. But at last they came to a high ridge— the other side of the valley—and there they found a treeless stretch, an area of new grass, brownish patches, and fallen trees. It was a place that showed signs of having been cleared by a forest fire.

At this point Tyrkir called a halt. "There are woods on all sides. If we cross this place, and if anyone happens to be watching nearby, they will see us."

"The answer is simple," Rigg said. "I will go across while you wait here and watch. If no one challenges me, you come ahead."

"I suppose there is no other way."

Rigg had no intention of walking casually across that open space. It was not at all like strolling along the beach by the Viking camp. When Tyrkir concealed himself, the boy took off helter-skelter. He ran, zigzagged, and ducked, managing to traverse a considerable part of the field that way. He was just beginning to feel the sheer joy of moving fast again, the pleasure of not being confined in the deep woods when, all of a sudden without warning, the ground gave way beneath his feet.

He went crashing down, banging his clenched fists against the rough edges of a fearsome pit, smacking hard on the bottom, which seemed all stones and rough wood. He lay dazed and in pain. It was as if a Viking axe had dealt him a fierce but glancing blow. Gingerly he moved his neck, while with outstretched arms and legs he struggled to feel out the damage to his body.

After a while, drifting in and out of consciousness, he was aware of the face of Tyrkir floating far above him. The old man was calling to him, moving about as if in another realm. For a minute Rigg's shocked mind conceived the notion that the rune master was actually flying while he, poor Rigg, was sinking farther and farther into the deep earth.

Then blackness came, and he passed out and remembered nothing more.

# The Huts by the River

A long time passed before Rigg came back to consciousness. The shock of the fall had seemed to sever his mind from his body, but slowly, after moments of ringing pain and spells of blank uncertainty, he drifted down from somewhere and was back.

He blinked and forced himself to move his fingers, then his arms. Next he tried to move his legs, but pain shot through his body. Blurred images floated before him, all streaked with dazzling light. He groaned and tried to focus.

At the end of a long tunnel he saw a blue smear of sky, wobbly, unfocused, dotted with small puffs of white smoke. *Clouds*, he thought, *the white smoke is really clouds*. He continued to stare upward, desperate to remember.

Rigg was in a pit, a trap, and he knew he had had a terrible fall. Light had descended and swallowed him, a blinding light in which he had seen a host of accusing faces. The faces had been very human, except that they were painted bright red. They had peered down at him, then some heads had floated together and talked for a while in low voices in a language he could not understand. The heads had disappeared and he had heard voices in the distance, one of them familiar, that of Tyrkir.

*Tyrkir,* he thought, *what has happened to Tyrkir?*

He stirred, and the pain shot through his back and thighs again. Nonetheless, he was able to move his arms and legs just a little. These were good signs.

Rigg gazed up, taking in the rough walls of the pit, the stones and the wood, the tufts of grass. Earth and rock enclosed him; the sky was a circular heaven, a Valhalla of blue promise, the clouds were feather-light. They seemed close enough to touch, and they raised his spirits. He must find his way out of here. He must stand in the open fields. He must hide in the deep woods.

*The red men are coming for me,* he thought. *I must make the effort now.*

Rigg unclosed his fists, flattened his hands on the rough floor, and pushed up with his right hand. Painfully he rolled himself over. He was on his side now, staring at one broken end of his longbow. It must have smashed when he hit the ground; it might well have broken his fall. His leather helmet had also split apart. He was lucky.

Slowly he drew his left leg in and pushed on his left knee and elbow, raising his head and his right shoulder from the rocky floor. The circular pit that enclosed him spun around; he felt sick but knew he had to continue. He closed his eyes and waited.

After a while he did the next thing. He pushed on his left elbow and, using his right hand as a lever, came up to a sitting position. Another wave of nausea engulfed him. He closed his eyes and waited.

Now he had to roll over onto his knees. This he did without mishap. His whole body ached mightily, but there were no sharp pains to suggest he had broken anything vital. At last he stood up, wobbling like a faulty tent pole, and nearly toppled over. But it was all right. He leaned on the rough wall, digging his fingernails into the soft earth. Once again he waited.

His head cleared. He managed to discard the shattered longbow. His sword had clanked down with him in the fall and was still in place in its scabbard. Things could be a lot worse. Still, he had to get out of there. He looked up, a dizzy spell came, but he fought it off.

There was only one way to get out of the pit. He must climb out. In his present condition it might just be impossible, but he had to try, and to begin with he had to get his body ready.

For the next fifteen minutes Rigg went through a series of exercises, stretching and bending, jumping, turning, and moving his battered body for all he was worth. It was painful enough, but amazingly, after all that effort he felt better, although he wanted badly to sit down again, to lie on the floor of the pit and rest. But he dared not allow himself that luxury. It would have been too tempting to remain there, perhaps to fall asleep.

Instead, he inspected the walls again. As he had noticed from the first, they were rough and uneven. He was in a deep pit, possibly dug in an earth fault of some kind, and carefully covered with matted grass—an animal trap set by the red men, possibly for him and Tyrkir.

He began the slow ascent, finding a foothold and a handhold and using his sword as a kind of long wedge, driving it into the soft earth, then pulling himself up by means of it, where he could. Although he made several false starts, plunging down unexpectedly, but not actually falling, he was able by this means to reach the very top of the pit.

When his head came over the edge and he saw the grassy fields and the woods rising beyond—and no red men in sight—he murmured a prayer of thanks to Odin, then with one last push catapulted himself upward and landed sprawling in the dust and the sunshine.

*The sword is lost*, he thought, *but there is no time to worry.*

Rigg tossed away his scabbard and sprinted at once toward the thicket where he had last seen Tyrkir. He did not even think of where the place must be; his instincts took him straight there.

As he had feared, there was no sign of the old man.

Rigg saw footprints everywhere and, when he made a close search of the trampled grass, he found an old worn Viking coin, an Arab dirham such as Tyrkir was accustomed to carry. There was no doubt about it: the red men had captured the rune master and had taken him off somewhere. And soon they would be returning to bring him in, too.

The first thing to do, he knew, was to get out of there. He was tempted to make his way straight back to the Viking camp to try to get help, but then he thought better of it. There was no time for that—Tyrkir was in danger. It was all up to him.

Rigg remembered a saying of Leif's: *When in doubt, do the unexpected.* Very good advice. And now, instead of running away, he would track the red men and find out where they had taken Tyrkir. No doubt they would have the advantage, since they knew this forest and had already snared him once, but he, too, was skilled at woodcraft. He had something to prove now, and he was determined to do it. That he had no weapons was worrisome; on the other hand, it meant that he would travel light.

The trail, in fact, was not very hard to follow. The red men must have been confident that they had only two adversaries to concern themselves with—both of them already snared—because they had made little effort to conceal their passage.

The tracks led away from the clearing, down into the next valley and inland from the sea. Rigg followed the trail directly, always on the lookout for sentinels or roving scouts. From time to time he stopped to listen, watching at every moment for signs of some presence in the woods. The rabbits that scurried across his path, the hawk hovering above, the rush of the wind in the trees—all these reassured him. Nothing seemed amiss, nothing touched by any human presence but his own.

It was after a good half hour's trek, when Rigg's aching body began to protest and he was sorely tempted to lie down in the nearest thicket, that he first heard the drums. The steady throbbing slipped into his consciousness with such ease and naturalness that at first he was almost unaware of it. He found himself tramping along in a kind of rhythm and suddenly realized he was marching to a beat. Stopping, he took note, then smelled the smoke.

He was coming down into the heart of the valley. Around him was the dark wall of the forest, a living barrier of gigantic trees rising to touch the sky. Rigg halted and heard voices in the distance, a prolonged chant that made him shiver with awe and apprehension. He seemed to take in for the first time what that sound meant, what his whole experience signified: that the Vikings were not alone and would never be alone in this new country, that they shared it with a strange race that spoke an unknown language and had customs well adapted to this brooding place. What were the odds of his being able to rescue Tyrkir? Very slender, he figured, similar to the odds that the Vikings could actually survive in this country. That was something to tell Leif, who had no idea that Vinland was peopled with such a strange red race, no idea of what power he might be up against if he decided to settle here.

Rigg no longer hurried through the thickets. He crawled forward a little bit at a time, rested, listened, and then moved again. Eventually he came down a narrow gully to a place where a huge boulder rested against the sloping hillside. Behind the boulder was a tiny space, perhaps an abandoned lair of a small animal. It was packed with dried-out leaves from the previous autumn, and when Rigg scooped these away, he saw that it would make an ideal place to hide and rest. He badly needed the latter, but now the drums and voices were very close. Rigg decided he would have to take a look before he lay down and made plans to rescue Tyrkir.

Painfully, step by step, he climbed the great boulder. At the top he gained a foothold from which at last he could see beyond the enclosing forest. When he did so, he murmured thanks to Odin for leading him to such a perfect place.

Before him lay a wide stretch of open land; there, shining in the sunlight stood a circle of domed huts. Smoke plumes trailed above the huts, rising against the background of the forest. Red men, a few women, and even some small naked children—who were not red-hued at all, but scarcely different in colour from any Viking child—moved in and out of the tents and between the huts and the river.

Rigg wondered if it was some quality in the shimmering sunlight that caused the scene before him—the people, the dwellings, the vivid clothing, the tiny boats by the shore—to make such a harmony within the dark greens, browns, and deep reddish tints of the natural setting. Or was it the drums, the odd voices, and the unexpected movements of the figures that turned the busy scene into something resembling a vivid but harmonious dream?

He watched and considered, but the dreamlike quality of his experience was suddenly shattered. A tall red man dressed in buckskin and wearing a feathered bonnet came out of one of the huts. He was leading another man along by means of an improvised collar and leash. The man, although he did not resist, moved with a certain air of affront. He peered about incredulously, as if he were surprised and also outraged simply by being where he was.

It was Tyrkir, and although he was shocked at the sight of his old friend made prisoner, Rigg also smiled with relief, seeing that the rune master was not only unharmed but resisting his powerful captor at every step.

# ᛏᛪᛁ ᚾᛁᚤᛪᛏ ᚢᛁᚤᛁ
# The Night Vigil

Tyrkir was alive! Rigg slipped off the rock and tumbled back among the leaves of the small cave. He knew that from his position between the boulder and the hillside he could keep watch over the village and make plans to try to rescue the rune master.

Rigg's exertions and the tension of the past few hours had exhausted him, however, and he knew he must rest for a while in his bed of dry leaves. His sight of the red men had raised many questions in his mind. Clearly they were a human tribe, but what their customs were he could not even guess. Enemies they appeared to be, since they had trapped him and captured Tyrkir. Even so, they could have easily killed them both and had not done so. No doubt they believed they had caught him. Were they going to sacrifice them both later, put them to the torture, devour them? The red paint was not reassuring; it seemed to Rigg that only savages would paint their faces so. Yet these people were strong and worked efficiently, and he had seen formidable weapons.

Rigg was puzzled, but his speculations went no further.

Almost against his will he felt his eyes closing and a heaviness settle on them. Resignedly he drew his body into a comfortable position, lay unmoving for a while, and then drifted easily into sleep.

*He dreamed of Thor, the thunder god. Rigg was climbing up a high, bare hill to get a vision of him. It was a wilderness, hardly populated, like the Vinland the Good discovered by the Vikings, only much bleaker. Rigg was sure he must be in Greenland, but an old crone spinning cloth by the fire, a woman who looked very much like Leif's mother, crept up to the boy, pointed at the landscape, and whispered a single word: "Byzantium."*

*As Rigg climbed the hill, lightning flashed close, and an ancient tree crashed down. The rain fell in torrents, the swollen river burst its banks, and the ships of the red men went spinning and crashing into the rocks. In the distant sky Thor's laughter sounded.*

Rigg woke amid the crinkling and rustling of leaves. The dream had stopped. All around him was darkness, then a sudden flash of light. Rain poured down, splashing off the big rock, sluicing in through the gathered leaves. He was not dreaming now—this was a real storm—but perhaps both the dream and the rain were good omens.

The boy moved, his body aching all over as he groaned in pain, then he remembered where he was and the dangers that threatened him. He pressed his lips tightly together and peered out of the enclosure. A great black torrent gathered in the gully beside him, spilling over its banks and wetting the rock, the leaves, and the exposed roots of an old tree. Thunder rolled menacingly above him, lightning flashed around him, and the trees and bare hillside stood out in hallucinatory splendour.

Rigg breathed a prayer to Thor, moved out of the cave, and clambered up his guardian boulder. It was slippery, but he managed to reach the top. From there he knew he could see the village. The next lightning flash revealed for an instant the red men's huts, the boats, and the river, alive with foaming water, behind them. There was no sign of anyone—no guards or watch fires. The village seemed shut up, and Rigg concluded it must still be the middle of the night and everyone must be sleeping.

Even as he watched, however, catching what glimpses he could in the fitful light, something moved among the dwellings. A tall, lean, nearly naked figure walked with slow, graceful steps up the hill directly toward Rigg's hiding place. Thunder crashed over the woodlands. Rigg looked on in openmouthed astonishment as a flash of lightning revealed one of the red tribe, a young man of about Rigg's age and build, walking solemnly in his direction.

In a panic the Viking boy slid down from the stone and crouched in the tiny cave, waiting. Above the patter of the steady rain he imagined the tread of footsteps. The youth drifted by in the darkness, walking straight up the gully beyond him. The intermittent lightning illuminated the passage of this stranger up the hill. He made a ghastly figure, his skin pale in the shivering brightness, his walk resembling that of a person in a trance.

Rigg crouched in his hiding place, wet and cold and trembling, unable to be certain whether he had seen a human being or a ghost. The Vikings often told stories of the animated dead, the *gengånger*, or zombies, those who walked the earth because their affairs remained unfinished. They also believed that the *fylgja* or fetch, the semblance of a living person, might appear at certain moments. But the strange being who walked slowly up the hill and into the forest—whose likeness did he bear?

Rigg, although frightened, had an overwhelming impulse to follow. He glanced down the hill to make sure no one else stirred in the village, then scrambled up the gully after the strange youth, taking cover behind each available bush and trying not to slip on the stones or the wet grass. Despite the darkness, the weather, and the unfamiliar terrain, it was not difficult to track the young red man. He walked, it seemed, oblivious to his surroundings, gliding through the woods without appearing to hesitate, never stopping or looking back.

They had gone scarcely half a mile up the winding path and through the drizzle and the darkness when the young man finally slowed his pace, hesitated, and then changed direction. The storm was abating a little, but a few lingering flashes of lightning, a few drumrolls of distant thunder, disturbed the eastern sky.

Rigg watched as the youth moved into the darkness. He followed warily, fearful of an ambush, then stopped when he heard close by a low, soft chanting, a voice making strange music in a language he did not know. Edging forward step by step, he sensed the presence of his quarry a few yards away, but at first he could not see him. He moved into some thick brush and stood, dripping wet from the rain, but secure from view. In the east the last faint flash of the lightning tore the sky, and he caught a glimpse of the other youth at last.

The stranger was seated cross-legged, his body stiff and straight, in a small clearing underneath a shelf of jutting rock. He looked very human and not at all like a ghost, and Rigg, who felt he might discover something of great importance about his enemies by doing so, decided to wait and watch.

Moving slowly and pausing from time to time to make sure he had not been observed, Rigg circled the clearing, gained a foothold on the rock, and climbed up into a small crevasse where a thick branch of an old maple grew right across the face of the cliff. Crouched on the stone, with the tree between him and the clearing, he could observe the seated youth and yet be relatively immune from discovery. Satisfied with this, he settled down to wait and watch.

A long time passed—Rigg was surprised later at how

much time. The strange youth did not move, but continued his chanting. He sat nearly invisible in the grey gloom, and after some hours his body seemed to melt into the land, while his voice continued, giving forth such a steady and impersonal music that it might have been, Rigg imagined, not the expression of a single person but the voice of this new land itself. Nameless sorrows, experiences of joy, the ancient life of the tribe—such things seemed to sound in that voice. Rigg, unclear exactly what was happening but sensing vaguely that he was witnessing something unique and magical, waited patiently in his hiding place.

Another hour passed. Rigg's alert curiosity and his sense that if he waited here something would happen began to give way to uneasiness. His perch was uncomfortable, and although the rain had stopped, the rock remained wet and slippery. Again and again he shifted his position, peering down into the clearing while his thoughts wandered back to the cave beside the village. He knew he should be getting back to his observation post there, that he should be planning his rescue of Tyrkir. The chant was hypnotic, and strange, and oddly soothing, but nothing was happening here. Surely it was time to move.

No sooner had Rigg come to this conclusion, however, than something else occurred, something that caused him to shrink back into his hiding place and give up all thought of changing places. On the hill path beyond where the youth sat, figures materialized in the gloom. Rigg could not see anything clearly, but he had grown so used to the semidarkness that an obscure change of pattern struck him and he was instantly aware of the intruders.

After some minutes, the figures moved and spread apart, approaching with a stealthy grace. Rigg could now see that there were four of them—four red men of the tribe, fully armed and walking up to the spot where the young man sat.

Taken aback, Rigg knew he must not move, that he hardly dared to breathe. The slightest movement would give him away, and now he had five men to deal with and not one. Escape would be impossible. At that point he came close to regretting he had crawled out of his cave, but at the same time he was intrigued and held by the scene below him. Were these intruders figures who had been called up somehow by the boy's chanting? Were they enemies who had come out of the woods to stalk and kill him?

The red men continued to approach, and soon they were well within the boy's line of sight, yet he showed no sign of being aware of them. He sat cross-legged, and his chant sounded as steady as ever in the gloomy forest shadows. The new arrivals might have been standing on the moon for all the boy seemed to care.

Rigg was puzzled by this, but what happened next astonished him. The men stood around the boy, a few yards from where Rigg crouched, circling the youth and pointing at him. They raised their voices in conversation, they laughed, one of them even kicked him lightly, without interrupting the boy's chant by a single syllable.

The men seemed, in fact, to be assuring themselves that the boy was impervious to their probing; once they had done this, they grew serious, nodded approvingly and, without any further intrusion, walked out of the clearing and slipped away down the path, heading in the direction of the village.

Rigg sat amazed, unable to fathom what all this meant. The boy's chant continued. The Viking youth bowed his head and waited.

# The Adversaries

Slowly, as the night passed, the darkness filled up with shapes, yet its contours seemed softer and more familiar, unthreatening. A slight wind rose and shook the leaves so that a sprinkling of water fell on Rigg's forehead and shoulders.

He was hungry and very tired, but felt he had now reached a state of quiet alertness, of peaceful attention. The chanting continued, close by in the darkness, and Rigg found himself closing his eyes for long spells to listen, shaping his own lips in silent imitation of that song.

The boy dozed and a series of images flashed through his mind. He was not asleep, but inwardly receptive, open, and no longer on guard or wary.

*He saw an eagle soaring above the forest and hills, the first morning rays of sunlight glinting on its wings. He saw an old bear stir in a cave and yawn. Then a single deer walked slowly up to the clearing and stood waiting. Rigg knew at once it was the very animal that had led him into the woods, the one that had allowed him to see the red demon.*

*"Now you understand," the deer said, and it was no surprise to hear the animal speak.*

It seemed then that the dawn came on very quickly, light flooding the eastern sky, making visible the far hills and the forest around him. At first the light was somewhat leaden and impenetrable, but with a curious and surprising speed it became more luminous and took on an almost unnatural hue. It was as if Rigg were looking at the trees and the paths through a blue darkness, through a haze of dark blue smoke, as if the light arose not from the sun but as a sustained burst of blue-white energy from within the trees and the grass and the stones themselves.

Rigg had an idea then. It seemed, at that moment, the most natural thing in the world. He suddenly abandoned his place of hiding, swinging away from the rock and dropping softly onto the turf. He stood a few feet now from the strange boy who had chanted through the whole night. Rigg walked up, as the four red men had done, and moved around him. The boy did not budge, nor did he stop his chanting. Rigg touched him on the shoulder.

The boy stood up. They circled and faced each other. He was almost exactly Rigg's height, with a long, narrow face, a high forehead, high cheekbones, and a strong, lean, agile body. Rigg reached out and touched the boy's cheeks. His eyes opened. They looked at each other for long seconds, Rigg's blue-eyed glance meeting the boy's darker gaze.

There was no hostility in the boy's expression or manner, but he stretched out both arms and held Rigg firmly by the shoulders. Rigg also stretched out his arms, and they began to wrestle, body matched with body in the blue darkness.

They wrestled cleanly and well. Rigg was an expert at this, and so it seemed was the other boy, who used his weight and his legs with great skill, forcing Rigg to hold on to avoid being thrown at once. Still clinging to each other, they fell together and rolled across the clearing. First one seemed to prevail, then the other, their bodies strained and tested, their muscles matched, the poise and balance of each exerted to prevent the other from gaining the advantage.

They rolled across the clearing until their bodies were covered with black earth and leaves. They grunted and murmured cries of strain or triumph, in turn, each in his own language. Repeatedly they got up, seized each other, and tried for the victory, but neither won it, neither could throw and hold the other, so that at last they had to stop. Both of them were exhausted, out of breath, sweating, covered in mud, but neither was defeated. They looked at each other for a few moments, eye to eye, then the strange boy simply sat down and resumed his chanting.

Rigg turned away and walked slowly down the hill path. The blue darkness had given way to the warm pink light of predawn. He seemed to be waking up, as if from a long dream. The night and the experiences of the night fell away like a dead skin. He felt changed and invigorated and found himself humming an old Irish song that his mother had taught him long ago.

It was only when he had nearly walked straight into the village that he realized the domed huts were full of men who would capture him and probably kill him. He ducked away into the trees, crawled a few paces through the soaking bush, and found his cave hideout. Crashing into the leaves, he promptly fell asleep.

When he woke up, a thousand thoughts flashed in his mind. The night's vigil came back to him, and he shook his head in wonder, rubbed his eyes, and took stock of his mind and his senses.

Had it been a dream, or had he really dared to come out of hiding and challenge the strange boy?

He had risked everything in doing so—that seemed

certain, at least to the logical mind. But he also knew he had experienced something to confound the logical mind, and that he had achieved a kind of victory, simply because he had challenged his enemy and held his own against such a strong and skillful adversary. Oh, yes, it had been real...

Rigg sat in his hiding place, feeling strong in mind and body. It was time, he knew, to rescue Tyrkir.

But how to do so? He decided to follow the path he had learned from the rune master and return to his dreams. On the previous night, in the middle of his dream about the god Thor, he remembered a single word spoken by one of his grandmothers, Leif's mother, the word *Byzantium.*

Now he used the technique Tyrkir had taught him and pondered the question: what could *Byzantium* mean?

Tyrkir, he knew, had ventured far to the east. He had been to the land of Rus and to the great Christian city— Constantinople—the bastion of Europe against the hordes of Asia. This was the old Byzantium, the capital of the eastern Roman empire, a corrupt city, Tyrkir had told him, but still a glorious one.

Rigg was puzzled, though. What had such a city to do with his task of rescuing his old tutor in this far-off wilderness? He closed his eyes and tried to remember all the things Tyrkir had told him about Byzantium, that holy, and unholy, city. He thought for a long time but could remember nothing that might apply to his predicament. Then he went back to his dream and thought of Thor and the lightning, and suddenly he had the answer.

Tyrkir had once told him a story about the people of Byzantium who had used a splendid and terrifying invention to overcome their enemies. It was a liquid substance that burned when it struck its target and was almost impossible to put out. This substance was called Greek fire, and they had shot it from tubes to destroy the Saracen ships in several great battles. This much Tyrkir had told him in his childhood tales.

Thor's lightning, the Greek fire—he must use the fire weapon against the red men. There was no way he could assault them with such a weapon, even if he had one, nor did he wish to, for it seemed to him a cowardly way of fighting. But what he might do—if he could only make fire—would be to distract them, to throw the village into confusion while he rescued Tyrkir.

But fire was not the only element in his dream. There was also water, and water, too, would serve him in his rescue. Even if he freed Tyrkir, they would be no match for the red men in the woods. But down beside the village was a fast-flowing stream, and those bark boats beside the stream looked like formidable craft. Like all Vikings, Rigg was an excellent sailor. The water route was their only hope of escape.

Rigg was satisfied with his ideas, but he knew he must be patient. His only hope of surprising the people of the village was at night. He decided to lie low in his cave until darkness fell and then to make his attempt.

The Viking boy was hungry and had only a few scraps of food left. There were no berries nearby, and already the village was up and active. Two small parties of men slipped past his hiding place and headed up the path toward the clearing where he had wrestled the young man. Remembering now the four red men who had surrounded the boy on the previous night, it occurred to Rigg that they might have been returning from an expedition to the northeast, an expedition that had been meant to recover him from the pit trap and bring him back to the village. By now, however, they would have reported on Rigg's escape, but what the village tribe would do when it heard that news, Rigg had no idea.

The village boy, Rigg was sure, would say nothing about their encounter, even if he remembered much. Rigg struggled to understand his own inner certainty about this. He told himself that their meeting had been on another plane—half dream, half reality. It had touched the spirit world and had been part of that process of initiation that Tyrkir had often hinted at, but which Rigg had previously never understood. Among the Vikings one did not talk very much about such private experiences. He would never reveal, for example, what spirit animals had appeared to him as he had sat there in the woods. They were his personal possession; he would meditate on them and learn whatever wisdom they could teach him. If the village boy did the same with his own animal guides, if he felt the same way about their meeting, then Rigg had nothing to fear from him. Nothing to fear, because they had waited and watched together, wrestled, almost shared a song. All this had made them brothers, kin in that other realm, that rare space where men did not seek to destroy in order to prove their power.

Now, as Rigg waited in the cave and attempted to suppress his hunger, he had much to think about, much to meditate on. Even so, the day seemed very long. Once he climbed up on the rock and watched the huts, only to find some village children playing a game with sticks, one that brought them closer and closer to his hiding place. If they saw him, they would be sure to sound the alarm. How close would they come? Would he have to try to retreat and hide in the deeper woods? But, just as his worst fears seemed to materialize, the children were dragged away to the village by some of the elders, and Rigg remained where he was.

All this time there was no sign of Tyrkir, a fact that worried Rigg greatly. Yet he continued to wait and watch. Sometimes he dozed a little. Then, just when it seemed it would never happen, the light began to fade and another night unfolded.

"Two days before the Vikings sail," Rigg said aloud to himself.

ᚠᛁᚱᛖ ᚼᚾᚼ ᛈᛁᛏᛁᚱ
# Fire and Water

Darkness settled on the forest. Rigg slipped out of the narrow cave and began a slow, painful crawl through the underbrush. The sight of a few twisting threads of smoke on the far side of the village had given him an idea, and he had decided to circle the camp and come out upstream. *Fire and water*, he reminded himself, *fire and water*.

An owl cried nearby, and bats zigzagged away toward the river. The moon rose, a real presence: leaves and branches glittered silver, half-hidden paths and trails floated up like the webwork of dreams.

Rigg crawled through the bush, his fingers touching willow scrub, the rough, wet bark of fallen trees. He could hear the river, the night birds, voices that sounded fearfully close in that darkness, laughter and the squalling of a few children. He could smell the roasted meat, too, and it made his stomach ache with hunger.

He crawled farther, but it seemed that Loki the trickster kept moving the river away from him, that the wily god had strewn soft, marshy land all along his path, steered him mercilessly toward every bramble bush, that he had conjured up voices behind every tree, padded footsteps on every cursed path.

Rigg had begun to doubt the wisdom of his circuitous approach. He longed just to stand and stride forward, but success meant caution, and he stayed on his hands and knees until at last he was able to crawl out on a rock shelf close beside the roaring river. From there he could see the village fires, which now lay well to his left. There were no guards, or stray villagers in sight. The first part of his plan was accomplished.

Quickly he scrambled down onto a narrow beach, gritted his teeth, and pushed into the icy water. Although he had thought himself prepared for it, the current flung him forward with abandon. He had to exercise all his skill, twisting and flattening his body and pointing his hands in the right way, to stay close to the shore where he wanted to.

He was hurled forward by the current, drenched and chilled to the bone, but he kicked out his arms and legs and finally floated steady, making his peace with the motion of the river. An old Viking pastime, one he had learned in childhood, served him well. He swam underwater, holding his breath, coming up only at intervals, yet it took all his skill just to stay close to the near shore. *I could drown here*, he realized, *but I won't let that happen.*

In mere seconds, it seemed, he was scraping on hard pebbles, banging his elbows on small stones and drooping branches, reaching out and snagging a fallen trunk that could easily have knocked his brains out. He used the dead tree to steady and hold himself.

*Never treat the water like a thrall*—an old Viking saying that he understood now better than ever.

Rigg swung himself up and managed to perch on the toppled trunk. He shook his body like an otter and blinked at the stream that boiled and glittered in the wild moonlight. His confidence swelled when he made out, not far away, the two things he had counted on: some village boats tied to a tree stump, and beyond them, the mushrooming shapes of the bark huts, smoke rising lazily from their domed roofs.

Voices, laughter, moving shadows—so close now he hardly dared breathe—yet he was exactly where he wanted to be. Knowing he had to work quickly, he turned his attention to the boats. They were bark canoes, complete with long paddles, odd craft high-set fore and aft and curving upward amidships, but to Rigg's experienced eye they looked sturdy, even seaworthy, and he was certain he could handle them.

Edging his way along the shore, he approached the canoes and snuggled in behind them. He now had a better view of the nearby huts, and was in sight of the rest of the village, strung out as it was along a winding, well-trodden path. It was from there that the voices seemed to come; it was there that the big fires blazed. The huts close by were quite silent and, if his suspicions were correct, empty of villagers.

He found that the nearby shore was pockmarked with tiny holes made by nesting animals, and noticed gaps in the bank where a few trees had toppled. Swiftly, with an energy born of desperation, he groped in these recesses for leaves, branches, and bits of wood, then piled all the dry material he found there into one of the canoes. He accomplished this as quietly as possible; even so, he paused now and then, crouched down, and listened. At one moment, to his amazement—he hoped he wasn't imagining it—he thought he heard, among all the alien accents, Tyrkir's familiar voice.

In a few minutes he had the canoe prepared as he wanted, piled up with dry brush, sticks, and leaves. But the next step was far riskier. On all fours again he crawled toward the nearest hut, put his ear against the wet bark, and listened.

It seemed empty, and he began to peel away some strips at the base of the structure. This was more difficult than he anticipated. All the material seemed well locked together, but just when he was once again cursing Loki the trickster, and quite ready to give up, he found a key strip. With a stone he had sharpened earlier, and carried in his belt, he made an aperture that was large enough for him to peer inside. What he saw was a dim, smoky interior. It was like looking into an antechamber of the underworld, he thought, yet at the same time he was reassured, since the hut appeared to be unoccupied.

Rigg worked feverishly and made the opening larger. The hut shifted and trembled a little—he hoped it would not collapse—but this caused him to work all the faster, and soon he had a space wide enough to crawl through. Taking a deep, solemn breath, he pushed his way into the enclosure and stood; it was a great relief to do so. No more curses were directed at Loki now. Instead he murmured his heartfelt thanks to Surt, the keeper of fire. His guess had been correct: this was a meat-smoking hut. Long strips of caribou steak hung from the roof and, wonderful to behold, a tiny fire burned on the earthen floor.

He was so hungry that he grabbed a few strips of the meat and devoured them. The chewy stuff was delicious. He thrust a few more such trophies into his belt, then seized the largest of the bark shingles. Using this and another smaller one as a prod, he slid some of the precious fire into his improvised brazier. Then, wasting no time, he retreated to the shore and collapsed beside the canoes. He had heard something—voices drifting closer—or was it his imagination?

*Not his imagination.* Two red men appeared suddenly on the path thirty feet from where he crouched. Tall, straight-backed figures wearing black kirtles, or skin doublets belted at the waist, clothes that eerily resembled the Vikings' own everyday dress, they walked in the clear moonlight and appeared so close to Rigg that he fancied he could read the expression in their remarkably large eyes.

When the pair stopped suddenly in the path and bent their heads together, Rigg tensed and measured his distance from the nearest canoe. How could these seasoned woodsmen fail to see his flickering fire, a flame that now seemed to him as large as a volcano's? Yet the men did not cry out; they were not even looking in Rigg's direction. Then, all at once, they burst out in a kind of chanting song, pointed up at the round moon, and laughed heartily together. Slapping each other on the shoulders, they laughed some more, then turned away and walked back down the path.

Rigg, hesitating no longer, sprang into action. He lifted his shingle of fire, set it carefully into the canoe and, standing knee-deep in the water, shoved the boat forward with all his might. The current took it at once. The leaves and dry bits of wood had already ignited, and flames started to spread across the boat from end to end.

Leaping into another canoe, Rigg seized one of the paddles and skimmed along behind the first boat. He stayed close to the bank and prayed that the prepared craft would ignite to some splendour. He was not disappointed. Turning and drifting, and gathering speed, the first canoe shot into the middle of the river. Flames flared up, light blazed on the water. To add to the effect, Rigg raised the berserk cry, ducking low in his canoe and staying close under the overhanging branches.

He was nearly opposite the village when the red men reacted. Several of them ran down to a small beach that lay beside the main group of huts. They shouted and pointed and peered back up the river.

Rigg landed his own canoe, sprang out, and sprinted through the trees and into the heart of the village. Women goggled from the huts, children ran away, their large eyes fearful. One man yelled and pointed, but no one hindered Rigg's desperate charge.

"Greek fire! Tyrkir!" the boy shouted. "Greek fire!" He twisted and turned, ducked around the huts, and kept in motion. There were more faces, a few laughing youths, the older men drifting up from the camp beach, but no sign of the rune master.

"Tyrkir!" the boy shouted.

Rigg was getting desperate. A young man took a spear and tossed it lazily in his path. Rigg stopped in his tracks to pick it up. A small crowd of men ascended from the main beach. Many, however, stayed behind, marvelling at the fire on the river. It would dawn on them any minute, Rigg feared, that it was one of their boats that was burning.

Then Tyrkir stepped out of a nearby hut and gaped at him. "I have been napping," he said, smiling.

Rigg grabbed him and led him away from the village path. They stumbled and cursed through the moonlit darkness. A few children ran after them, shouting. Two young men made a real effort to stop them. Rigg swung his spear and knocked one down; the other ducked away and shouted something to the village men.

"I have a boat," Rigg told the rune master.

The old man nodded. He was moving faster now; he seemed to have woken up to their danger.

The canoe rocked fearfully, and Rigg had some difficulty getting the rune master into it. But the boy held on and, leaning his weight on the rocky bank, settled in behind the old man.

"Use the paddle I brought for you!" he shouted. "We've got to get out of here."

The rune master fumbled in the darkness. Rigg groaned, but together they stroked the boat out into the fast current. A crowd of villagers ran along the shore, shouting at them and pointing. There was much confusion, and one man, standing knee-deep in the river, kept repeating a phrase and pointing to the burning boat.

When Rigg and Tyrkir came opposite the village beach, the man screamed and waved his arms. A couple of red men ran out and fired arrows that swished across the bow. Within seconds they had left the burning craft behind. It was quite a sight, Rigg thought, pouring out smoke and just beginning to douse and settle.

Now the air had grown acrid and thick, but they bent their heads, held their breath, and paddled harder. In a few minutes they were clear, and the river stretched before them, a dark stream mottled with silver light.

"Good work," Tyrkir muttered. "A miracle, in fact. But I think they will come after us."

# ᚺᚾᛏᚺᛖᛏ ᛁᛏᛞᚺᛏᛁ
# Ancient Stones

The bright moon struck silver in the rushing water. Under the Vikings' skilled hands the canoe raced forward, following the river as it swept through the forest, then into a narrow defile whose steep sides shut out the light. After a dangerous run through miles of swirling rapids, the canoe emerged in a gentle run of meadows, tufted with grass and as smooth as a soft wool blanket.

"I think we've left them behind," Rigg said.

"For the time being," the rune master told him. "They are not hysterical people. They will think about things, make their plans, and follow us when they please. In this land all the advantages are theirs."

They pulled their canoe up to a low bank and ate some of the cold strips of venison. Neither wanted to risk a fire, so Tyrkir sat shivering in his cloak, but his eyes shone as sharply as ever in the now-fading moonlight.

"You and I were separated only a short time," Tyrkir said, "but I think I have learned a little about these people. Everything about them surprises me. They are not demons or savages. They are not even very violent. I do

70

not think they would have killed us. If they come after us, it will be to get their boat. Perhaps they are angry because you destroyed another boat. Most of all, though, I think they are curious. They may think we dropped from the moon, or arrived from some other world."

"But we thought something like that about them!"

"Yes. The older I get the more I realize what strange ideas can get into human skulls. The world is mysterious, that I believe, but the mysteries are seldom where we look."

Rigg nodded thoughtfully, then told the rune master about his experience in the woods and of his wrestling match with the strange boy. He did not disclose his dreams or the dream animals that had appeared to him, but he let Tyrkir know something of what he had felt as he walked toward the village after the wrestling match.

"I wasn't afraid of the red men then," he confessed. "I felt almost as if I were walking into my own village. I had to stop myself and remember to hide, because I knew I had to rescue you."

"Your mind was serene, Rigg, and you judged well. That boy might be a shaman in training. He might have been seeking contact with the animal spirits. I will not ask you what you saw there, but I know we are not the only people to meditate and to seek hidden truths in order to follow a good life path. I have seen things in the East...but we must move on now. We must travel somewhat farther before sunrise. This would be a poor place to have to conceal ourselves."

Wearily they launched the canoe again, floating out into the darkening stream. On the broad meadows the current had slowed a little. They coasted gently forward. The land rose around them mile by mile, and soon the river narrowed, winding its way through a deep cleft in the rocky cliffs.

"Where is this taking us?" Rigg wondered aloud. His hands were sore and all the muscles bruised in his fall into the pit seemed to protest now. "Is it possible we'll float into some waterfall or drift into an underground lake and be lost forever?"

The rune master scoffed. "I saw whalebones and sealskins among the huts. The village people must visit the seashore. In summer they could find abundant food there. This river may flow out to the sea, and we will not starve or be lost if it does. But I think we must rest and sleep here."

Some trees had fallen across the river, creating a tangled bank of boughs and driftwood that formed a pool large enough to manoeuvre in. One side of the pool lapped at a rock shelf, several feet across. The walls, beetling black in the sombre light, overhung the low shelf. It did not seem to Rigg a very happy place, but he was tired and eager to rest.

They found a small roll of thong in the canoe, unrolled it, and tied the boat to one of the branches, then huddled in the rock cleft. It was one of the most uncomfortable beds Rigg had ever tried. Nonetheless, he soon drifted into a fitful sleep.

He was awakened by the screaming of a bird. A hawk must be drifting through the grey morning sky, he decided, although he could see nothing from where he lay. His bones ached, and it was almost too painful to move, but he compelled himself. Crouching on the rock ledge, peering upward, Rigg could see how the cliff sides glowed faintly with the first light. He reached over and shook the rune master into a grumbling state of consciousness. The old man rolled over, yawned, closed his eyes, and reminisced.

"I was dreaming about a bed where I once slept in a house in Constantinople. That bed was stuffed with eiderdown, I had sheets made of silk, and my covers were blankets of the finest light wool. The baths were wonderful there, not like ours, but warm and inviting, like the sauna. Steam warmed your skin until it was as tender as a doe's hide. It was a soft city, one that pampers and spoils good men, but sometimes a little comfort is welcome."

They sat there shivering and munched unhappily on the last of the venison, then once again launched the canoe. Paddling quickly away from the rock defile, they kept turning, casting apprehensive glances behind them. Since the steep banks curved sharply and the river behind them was hidden, they feared they would not see their pursuers until it was too late.

Soon, however, the river churned up mightily and jagged rocks threatened to tear the canoe's hull apart, forcing them to attend to their steering. At the same time they emerged from the canyon and once again entered a forest realm: low, rolling valleys surrounded them, emblazoned now with the first fierce rays of sunshine. There was much bog land, brown and grey stumps and fallen spruce, and ducks rising in alarm as the paddles stroked the water. On the higher reaches balsam stood in mighty stands. They saw paper birch, aspen, alder, pin cherry, and mountain ash. Then the river again ran level and they made an easier passage. Here the air was clear and fresh and they began to get a whiff of the sea.

Where the river flowed into a tiny lake, they beached the canoe and rummaged for berries in the thickets. As they stood on the wet sand, their hands smeared with dark red juices, Rigg heard a sound that made him turn his eyes northward. Scanning the sky, he saw a dark cloud, a twisting rag of uncertain substance and shifting contours, half ignited by the blazing sunlight. It approached them steadily all along the line of the northern horizon.

Rigg blinked at the apparition, then stood back stunned as his ears, sharper than the old man's, monitored the sound. It was a low clanking, like a set of deep notes on a minstrel's harp, twanging and reverberant. It was one of the strangest sounds he had ever heard, and he remembered it from the previous year at the Viking camp—a sound that had brought everything at the settlement to a standstill, made all ears hearken, and turned every eye on the sky.

Now Tyrkir heard it, too. "The wild geese," he murmured, and they stood together, watching the great flocks approaching, myriads of them, dark shapes flashing in the sunlight, an unceasing counterpoint of voices, the sky crammed with them, the long V-formations strung out across the horizon, heading south, away from the winter and the cold north.

As Rigg watched with breathless attention, the legions of birds passed over. At that moment he felt—far more even than when he had seen them that spring flying north over the Viking encampment—that he was a privileged witness to the enactment of one of the miracles of the earth and of the great mother. His experiences in the forest, and his encounter with the red men, had changed his perspective. He himself had turned around and was flying all at once in a different direction. How could he any longer feel himself to be a stranger in this wild land?

Rigg said a few words in gratitude to Freya, earth goddess, and to Odin, the god-magician who drinks at the stream of Mimir at the roots of Yggdrasill, the world tree. He thanked these powers, and the unknown powers of this land, for allowing him to be present at this perfect moment.

When the birds became a mere line on the southern horizon, a great silence descended on the travellers. With splashing oars, Rigg and Tyrkir paddled until they found the narrow passage that ran out of the lake. They steered between the reeds and high banks through another grove of black spruce. Some time went by and they drifted lazily along. There was no sign of pursuit and they felt reassured, but the river was growing shallower and they feared they might have to abandon the canoe altogether, for it was far too large for them to drag across a portage.

While they were exchanging anxious thoughts on this, the river left the forest completely and flowed into a broad, flat plain. They drifted past the low scrub fields and, on either side, saw several mounds, mere hummocks, covered by berries and dwarf alders. Behind these tumuli were a few scattered clumps of giant spruce, while a ridge of low hills shut in the plateau many miles distant.

When the first two or three monuments appeared, they seemed perfectly natural, part of the landscape, spiky stones jutting up from the meadows, like fingers pointing at the zenith of the sky. But soon Rigg saw a few more of them, lying in a large space past the earthen mounds, giant stones, like the eggs of fabulous birds, balanced on smaller ones that must have been placed there to support them.

"What *is* this place?" Tyrkir questioned. He turned to Rigg with a shrug, and they paddled on, but much more slowly.

An atmosphere had invaded the plain. Rigg felt it, but put it down to the clouds that had just then swept unexpectedly across the sun. However, when the sky brightened minutes later, the atmosphere persisted.

Rigg and Tyrkir looked at each other. They let the canoe drift slowly to the shore and, without a word, both climbed out. When the boat was secured, they walked slowly back among the mounds and the raised stones, which were of two kinds. Some were tall pillars, twelve or fourteen feet high and as thick as the trunks of very old trees, chiselled and hewn as if from a cyclopean original. Others were huge boulders, so large in girth as to make them look almost absurd on their tiny stone props.

Both kinds of monuments—for Rigg had no doubt that was what they were—were spaced at a distance from the hillocks or tumuli, some of which also revealed traces of stonework. But the stone embedded in the tumuli gave a hint of ancient construction. Loose earth seemed to have been piled up, or must have blown in, to cover the frames of the buildings.

Rigg and the rune master walked in silence toward the nearest of the tumuli. Even though it was nearly noon, and the sun stood directly overhead, Rigg shivered a little. He was aware of how the wind rose from nowhere, how the grass tufts moved and dust blew up in their faces so that they choked and for a few minutes could not speak.

Tyrkir and Rigg watched the dust devils move across the plain, listening to the wind, feeling their clothes flap a little in the fitful breeze. Then the rune master said quietly, "This place has nothing to do with the village, or with the red men. The red men are alive and struggling. They are human beings. This is a dead place, a vast sepulchre, deserted long ago and left to the dead, or to the spirits of those who built it and vanished. This is a place of the old people, of the ancient settlers of this land. They, too, may have been human beings—once. But now they are merely presences, or memories. They have left something behind, though—a shadow world, one that clings to the buildings here, that springs out of this geometry of stones and seems about to break into our reality with a powerful force. And even the gods, even mighty Thor, powerful Freya, the wily Odin, want no part of this place."

Rigg nodded. As the rune master spoke, they had approached the largest of the mounds, a square, rugged pile of earth in which stone lintels and a few ancient posts could be seen, embedded in the crumbling tumulus like bones. This structure was larger than the main Viking booth, but flattened, topped by some rough brush and, to Rigg, indescribably desolate.

They came within a few feet of this mound and stood

silently under its sloping roof. Then they noticed, over-grown a little by moss and half covered by trailing vines, the figures carved on the face of the stone.

# Messages from
# Past and Present

Tyrkir stepped forward and pushed aside the trailing vines. Rigg began to scrape away gently at the moss. Slowly a row of deeply incised images emerged on the face of the stone. The weathering action of rain, summer heat, and winter frost had taken their toll, but the figures were clearly visible. Seeing them, Rigg stepped back, excited, awestruck at their discovery.

The wind continued to blow across the plain. The scrub plants, the trailing vines, the brambles and the branches of the spruce, moved and stirred in the clear sunlight. Dust trails rose from among the tumuli and the monuments. Two crows came shrieking and cawing from the other side of the river. Rigg waited for Tyrkir to finish the close inspection he was making of the incised figures and symbols.

From where he stood Rigg could now see that the apparently random distribution of the monuments and tumuli was an illusion. In fact, they were arranged in a semicircle, with the river serving as the straight side. The tapering stones made pairs with the boulders, while the hillocks, and the mounds that overlay the buildings, formed an alley or an axis in the centre of the enclosure.

"Circles," Tyrkir said quietly, also observing what Rigg had just noticed. "Circles and half circles—places of enclosure. This has never been a deserted land. People came here long ago and set up their sanctuaries. We are standing beside what must have once been a temple. Look at these inscriptions—a star, an earth sign, an image that looks like a pair of idols, and that one must be a ram or a sheep. It is picture writing. Yet these are not the same as the marks the red men made on the trees. I think they must be very old. I have seen something like them in the East, in ancient Egyptian scrolls. The Vikings are far from being the first people here! Even the red men may not be the first. This changes everything. We must tell Ivar and the others. They must know that the red men are not demons or savages. They came as settlers, as we might wish to. Or else they are descendants of the people who made these—people from the old lands, from Egypt, perhaps, or Africa. This is a long-settled country."

"But, Tyrkir, Ivar may sail tomorrow or the next day! And how will we persuade him to stay? We saw what happened to Helgi. Their fear will be stronger than our knowledge."

Tyrkir considered this for a moment. "It may be so," he said finally. "But I do not think they will sail without waiting a few more days for us. Your mother would hardly allow it. As for Helgi, I think that the red men approached him and that he died of fright—so I told them and so I believe more firmly than ever now."

"I don't think they want to kill anyone," Rigg said bravely, although even now he knew he could not be entirely sure of this. "They are as amazed at our presence as we are at theirs. Perhaps we can talk to them, trade with them, find out what they think."

"Yes, with the strength of the camp behind us, we

could do that. If we can convince Ivar and the others."

They walked together toward the river down the broad alley between the crumbling earthworks. Although fascinated by what they had seen, Rigg was anxious to get away from this place, where the sunlight seemed bleak and the wind soughed mournfully between the ancient stones. Who could tell what spells, what presences might lurk here? It was good to have seen all this, but even better to be moving on.

The sight of the ancient stones had brought back to Rigg his dream of the cave and the treasure. In that dream he had encountered something vague and yet frightening, something he had barely managed to escape.

The monuments spoke clearly of a land of ancient gods and nameless spirits, veiled and perhaps fearful presences of whom even the red men must stand in awe. These were the powers Rigg had sensed in his dream, and although they had remained invisible and mysterious, he had been aware of their sheer age and of their still-potent energy. Rigg wanted to learn more, to decipher the signs on the stone, to read the secret meaning in the geometric array of the monuments. The real treasure he sought, the one he would share with all Vikings, was knowledge. He would devote his life to plumbing the past, but he would do so with care and reverence. As Tyrkir had said, it was no good meeting the unknown with either fear or bravado. One had to have a clear vision and a steady heart, for the world was very old and the past was deep, much deeper than he had imagined, deeper even than anyone's dream of it.

They found the canoe and prepared to leave the place of the monuments, deciding they would look for food farther on. Although it was not spoken between them, Rigg knew that Tyrkir shared his feeling of unease, his sense of the bleakness, the inhuman aura, of this ancient setting. He was all the more startled then when the old man, who had been busy trying out his paddle in the water and balancing himself on the bank so as to once again board the canoe, stopped, raised his sharp gaze to the western horizon, and pointed.

Rigg turned and saw three round fat white puffs of smoke floating slowly upward, rising above the dark line of the trees and the low cliffs. Higher and higher they soared, then spread out, finally dissipating against the cold blue background of the sky. Rigg watched with fascination, then turned to Tyrkir for enlightenment.

The old man shrugged. "Not a natural fire. I am afraid it might be some kind of signal."

"Look there!" Rigg pointed to a position farther east and somewhat north of the plain of the monuments. There, too, smoke climbed the sky, this time in a shape that resembled an arrowhead, or the rune letter *Tiwaz*. It rose from a spot, not ahead of them, but considerably closer to them than the first signal. "Is it possible they are talking to each other, one group of red men telling the other something about our presence?"

As Rigg said this, Tyrkir shook his head, and a grim look came into his eyes. "I hope it is not so. Let us pray this river leads to the sea. I have a great longing to see the waves again. Now we must make haste before we are trapped in this place."

They pushed off and rowed mightily, but the river disappointed them. It grew narrower and shallower and then, not more than five miles from the place of the monuments, the boat scraped the bottom. They were in a small grove of trees, surrounded by catkinlike weeds and marshy swampland. Disappointed, they climbed out. The water trickled away over the pebbled streambed. A duck, squawking in the brush nearby, seemed to complain of their presence.

"There must be a way," Tyrkir said, and Rigg was quick to find it. It was a portage path between some alders, but clearly marked by the worn grass and signalled by a couple of pointing stones. "So there is hope," Tyrkir said. "But now we will have to work."

Rigg lugged the canoe, and Tyrkir helped as much as he could. It was not an easy portage for two such travellers, but at least the ground was level. They stopped several times to rest, and after the fifth stop they heard a welcome sound.

"It is another river—or this river, finding some life again," Tyrkir said. He wiped the sweat from his face with his old blue cloak, now very ragged.

They struggled along through the bush, the welcoming sound drawing them. After a while the ground underfoot grew spongy and damp, then a trickle of water appeared, running over the small white stones. They pushed aside some brush and saw another river, a broad, deep stream, running almost due east.

"Freya," Rigg murmured, thanking the goddess for this happy encounter.

They floated the canoe, fell into it, and stroked forward. The next hours were breathtaking. The stream ran into a narrow defile where, except for a thin band of blue directly overhead, the sky seemed to disappear. They flashed through dangerous rapids, soaked to the skin, the boat wheeling and turning so that they shouted contradictory orders at each other. The canoe seemed about to capsize, or to smash on the rocks, until Rigg turned the craft and held it just in time. They roared straight along and into a spectacular valley. Cliffs towered high above them, hawks circled, startled caribou, about to drink, sprang away.

The river ran on. There were many bends and slow passages, and they sensed a great descent, although at any moment there was almost no noticeable slope. When the valley broadened out to a plain, Rigg looked nervously about. He did not want any more of the monuments. But after some time they were in a forest again. It seemed to go on forever, and it was dark. They were tired and hungry, starving almost, but they refused to stop.

Long before it happened, they sensed what was coming. They had noticed the gulls wheeling above, sniffed the salt in the air. They had taken in the slight changes in the vegetation, heard, they imagined, the familiar crash of waves on shore. Every fibre of their bodies longed for it, and when at last the river turned in one final great loop and the vegetation thinned and disappeared, they saw how the sky ran down to the horizon, how the flat band of the foreshore was broken by the thrust of the river, and they knew they had done it.

They made one last powerful effort. The river ran into a small lagoon and beyond the lagoon the pure white waves came at them, as if in a greeting. They cheered and slapped each other on the shoulders. Rigg kept repeating, "The sea, the sea," and in the lagoon he abandoned the boat and did a joyful dance among the shells and the darting crabs.

"Be careful with the boat," Tyrkir said. "We will need it."

Later, after they rested, they hid the canoe. There were many signs on the beach that this was a main passage the red men used to reach the sea: a few broken implements, stone markers, even bits of an old smashed canoe, gradually rotting back into the sand and grass. They made a cold supper with the crab and a fish they had speared with the native weapon and concealed themselves among the dunes on the other side of the small lagoon. There they would be close enough to the boat to get it into the water before they could be intercepted. Rigg hoped that no one would find them, for he had no illusions about being able to outrun the powerful red men in one of their own canoes.

The night came on and Rigg breathed much easier. There was no sign of any pursuit. Tyrkir walked the beach and took note of the constellations; they could afford no mistakes in the morning. Rigg found it wonderful to lie on the edge of the sea and to listen to the waves pounding the long shore, to hear the frogs in the swamps and the birds in the marshes, to watch the glitter of moonlight in the water, and to know that they had left behind the forest, the red men, and the bleak plain with its ancient monuments.

Yet as he settled down among the dunes in his improvised bed of sand, leaves, and soft branches, Rigg thought about the next day's challenge. They must circle the great headland and make their way down the length of the fjord that would lead them back to their own beach and the Viking booths. Ivar and the others would wait for them—at least a few days—his mother would see to that. But what the others would say when they heard their story of the red men's village, the woods, and the monuments, Rigg could not guess.

He closed his eyes and woke up to the sound of the wind in the nearby groves. A light spray of rain touched his face. He dragged himself up and went to check the canoe, leaving Tyrkir snoring. As he gazed out at the slate-grey sea, at the dark mass of great curving headland, at the murky sky bending over the wrinkled water, Rigg thought of Leif far away, and of what news he would have to tell his father. Rigg had sensed there were mysteries abounding in this new land, which was really an ancient place, and now he had proof.

In a few hours they would test themselves once again on the sea. Rigg walked back to where they had hidden the canoe and began to drag it through the dunes to the edge of the water. When he was halfway down the sloping strand, the boy saw a figure rise from the shadows near the grove and hurry toward him.

He reached for the spear, which he had carefully stowed in the canoe with some berries and raw fish, but recognized Tyrkir coming over the sand with a haste that caused Rigg to scan the shore behind him for a pursuer. No one else appeared, the night's calm seemed unbroken, but the rune master came up, nearly breathless, laid his hands on the prow of the canoe, and pulled it forward.

"Someone is there, in the woods," he said. "I saw nothing, but I heard bird calls that seemed to me not like real birdsong. They were too regular and too calculated. Then I searched carefully and found some tracks in the moonlight—fresh tracks. We must shove off now or risk capture." Together they pushed the canoe into the water, seized hold of the paddles, and fought through the light breakers.

They were on the sea again, but the next several hours were full of tension. More than once they looked anxiously behind them, expecting pursuers, but none appeared. The shore was reassuringly empty, the beach, as the sun came up, a ribbon of gold. The sky had turned a rare blue; all around them the water was a chalice of magic light. The rocky headland stood out, a cyclopean wall, distant, but clear in every contour.

"We are lucky with the weather," Tyrkir said.

They paddled steadily, and at one point rested and ate some cold food. All the while they kept watch, but there was still no sign of pursuit. The day wore on. They drew near the cliffs, which towered above them like the ramparts of Utgard, citadel of the giants.

As they turned the headland, Rigg saw a figure standing motionless on a rocky shelf hundreds of feet above them. He called at once to Tyrkir, "Look, high on the cliff there, beyond that great chasm—a sentinel."

Tyrkir looked up and nodded grimly.

*A red man*, Rigg thought, *keeping watch on our return.* The figure's stillness—suggesting patience and control—was disconcerting.

They paddled on, and saw three more sentinels watching them from the rocky heights. Then, at last, they came into the fjord.

*Now*, Rigg thought, *now at least we are safe from the ocean, safe from any sudden storm or bad weather.*

They continued for another hour and were nearly exhausted.

"I can see the beach and the booths!" Tyrkir shouted.

Even as he spoke, something flared up close to the water, an object floating out in the bay, between them and the booths. It was a sudden illumination, like the first lighting of a fire, but on the surface of the water.

"I don't understand!" Rigg cried. "Are they sending us a signal?"

Tyrkir was silent for a moment, then turned slowly to Rigg and nodded. "In a manner of speaking perhaps," he muttered. "It is the funeral boat of Helgi."

# The Shape Shifter

Rigg opened his eyes. He was in a warm place, wrapped in skin blankets, listening to the sound of someone's heavy breathing. The room felt close and familiar, and flickering light danced on the earthen walls. He could smell pine boughs, smoke, and damp peat, and hear the sound of the waves lapping gently on the night shore. He was home.

He remembered a little of his return, how he and Tyrkir had waded ashore, staggered up the beach, and collapsed near the new Viking *knarr*. He remembered voices, exclamations, strong hands lifting him, how he had been carried to his bed, given a sip of warm milk—and then nothing more.

Memories flashed through his mind—of a deep pit in the forest, of a sky full of winged shapes. He remembered his midnight watch and how his patience, strength, and agility had been tested by one like himself, yet so different. He had rescued Tyrkir, and they had made quite a run from that beach on the other bay, around the point and into the fjord, past the flaming pyre that marked the last rites for poor Helgi. He would not forget that trip, and maybe even some *skald* would tell of it later at the hearth fire, how he and Tyrkir had seen the interior of the great forest, outrun the red men, discovered the writing on the ancient stones, and escaped to the sea.

But now Rigg's body was tired, and he was hungry. Aching arms, palms rubbed raw by the paddles, back cramped and stiff—these he could ignore—but not the hunger pangs that made his stomach twist. He yearned for a bowl of milk, a crust of bread, anything but raw fish and fruit.

Rigg groaned, stretched, and disentangled himself from the warm bedding. Tiptoeing across the cold floor, he peered down at the wooden frame on which old Tyrkir lay sleeping, smiled, and pulled the covers around the old man, Then, noticing that his mother's bed was empty, he slipped out of the room.

A figure rose out of the shadows. Fianna embraced him, held him for a minute, whispering his name, then drew him away to the low-burning central fire. "I was watching while you slept," she said. "Are you rested now? Are you hungry? Yes, I knew you would come back! I knew we would have this moment together."

Her joy shone in her glance as she immediately began to prepare some food for him. Two or three men huddled in beds in the far corner, snoring. Others were mere lumps in the darkness. Rigg and his mother spoke in whispers.

"Ivar would have sailed," she told him, "only the boat wasn't ready." Then, with a chuckle, she added, "I got Rolf the navigator to see to that. As you know, he's always gone far to please me. He's waiting for us by the new *knarr*. We must hear your story and decide what to do."

She held him for a moment by the shoulders, and he said softly, "I was so tired. I must have collapsed on the beach. How is the old man?"

"He's weary enough but well. And it's a good thing, because we'll need him tomorrow."

Rigg nodded, devouring the meat and hot porridge she had prepared for him. While he ate, he told her of their journey, of what they had discovered about the red men.

When he was finished, Fianna was silent for a while, then she nodded and said, "It must be true then that the Irish came here long ago, and others before them. The Vikings aren't the first. But the others must all have departed long ago. If the red men are so skilled and familiar with this land, then we must try to trade with them. They can help us. Are there many of them?"

"We didn't see very many, but I think there are a lot more in the woods, which seem to go on forever."

Fianna leaned forward and lowered her voice until it was barely a whisper. "Ivar is still full of fear. Every night he paces up and down and seems about to transform into a berserker and prowl the woods to kill. And he is determined to sail away. The red-painted faces of the people here will not reassure him. He won't believe they're human beings."

"But he *must* believe. We can do everything Leif imagined. We can get great riches from this country, and we can discover new things, learn great mysteries, but only if we work with the red men."

Fianna shrugged. Rigg finished his meal and they crept outside, anxious not to disturb Ivar and his cronies in the chieftain's room. They slipped away between the main booth and the shed in which the Vikings were making parts for the ship and also fashioning wood for the new vessel. Walking briskly, they moved on past the kilns and the smelting pit and another outbuilding that held the smithy, past the slag heap, then another shed, reeking of the fish that were still drying there. Eventually they came out on the long, narrow bar that divided the big lagoon from the open water. On that fateful hill where Rigg had sounded the alarm and Helgi had perished, a watch fire burned brightly in the silver night.

"There are two guards now," Fianna explained, "and no one will take the watch without a big fire."

On the curving beach before them Rigg saw the sturdy new *knarr*, propped on a wooden frame, and beside it the canoe he had stolen from the red men. Beyond, the wide bay and the great fjord looked peaceful and impassive, asleep in the moonlight, and utterly impervious to the little fears of men.

Out from behind the *knarr* stepped Rolf, the navigator, with his shiny bald pate and his kindly eyes. When he saw Fianna, he brightened. Embracing Rigg and clapping him hard on the shoulders, he said, "Well, lad, you did it. Ivar thought you'd perish out there, yet you came back, and Tyrkir, too. But things aren't well here. Thank heavens the ship is nearly ready. We'll soon drink a toast to Njord and his children in the horn cups and sail away. That will be a blessed day."

Sitting on the beach, they watched the waves roll in gently and cast tiny pebbles at their feet. Rigg explained as best he could his ideas about the red men. Rolf listened patiently, but afterward shook his head.

"It will never do," he said quietly. "Say what you will, they're savage men. How can we speak to them or know what they plan against us? They are many, we are few. Ivar will attack them, and the rest of the Vikings will follow. No, the best plan is to sail away and carry your news to Leif. If Leif comes back, that would be a different story. But I don't think he'll return now." Rolf glanced at Fianna, but she seemed undisturbed by his pessimism.

"Tyrkir will speak for us," she said. "And my son, who is a man now and has done a great deed, will speak for himself. Ivar will have to listen."

At that moment a strange growling sounded in the

faint moonlight. It was first a low bark, then a long, sustained moan. It might have been the voice of an animal, and yet there seemed also to be something human in it. Perhaps because of this, when the cry was repeated and became an eerie wailing that resonated on the low hills, Rigg's hair stood up on the back of his neck.

All three exchanged glances.

"It's Ivar," Rolf told them. "The moonlight has disturbed him and he's prowling the hill in his berserk shape. If he met one of the red men now, he'd have no words—nothing but the wolf cry. He'd kill anyone in his path."

Rigg got up and paced the beach. "I'll find a sword. Lend me yours, Rolf. We must kill Ivar before he brings us all to ruin."

Fianna shook her head, and Rolf fixed the boy with a searching look. "Why such talk? Has the chief infected you with his madness? Sit down, Rigg, and invoke the wisdom of the goddess. Be the clever-thinking warrior you were meant to be."

Chastened, Rigg sat down. But his blood was up and his heart was beating fast. He knew Ivar was a danger to them all. How could they deal with him?

"These people you call the red men," Rolf said. "I know they've been watching us. I saw them on the cliffs on the other side of the bay. Some of the men wanted to go after them, but Ivar wouldn't risk the small boat. He can be a sensible leader by day. It's only at night and in the moonlight that his berserk nature claims him, so far at least. And the moonlight will soon pass."

Rigg thought of his own night adventure, of his wrestling match in the deep woods. He had more kinship with the native boy than he did with his own leader. How calm the red men had been when their camp was invaded, and how efficiently they had pursued the canoe and set up watch on the Viking camp. Rolf was right: the Vikings would have to think clearly to deal with this danger.

Now the navigator stood and paced a few times before the red men's canoe. "A fine-looking craft, although strangely balanced. Did she run well, son?"

"She did."

Rolf nodded, considered for a while, then took Fianna by the hand and helped her to her feet. "Why not go back to the booth and get some rest? You'll need all your wits in the morning. Rigg can stay with me and nap on the beach. At dawn bring Tyrkir here and we'll make our plans together."

"If you'll promise me to watch this young hothead," Fianna said. "One wolf prowling the camp is enough."

They laughed quietly together. Then there was a pause and silence. The wolf growls had stopped a few minutes before but, distracted, they had not taken it in. Now they all listened together, but what they heard was not the grotesque and half-stifled cries of an animal, but the footsteps of an intruder coming toward them from the shadowy boxes and hide tarpaulins piled behind the *knarr*. Rigg stepped in front of his mother, while Rolf picked up the spear he had stowed among the sailing gear by his watch post.

Ivar, the chieftain, naked to the waist and wrapped in a coarse animal skin, stepped out of the shadows and confronted them. In his right hand he held his famous war axe, an ancient huge-bladed weapon. He glared at them, swung the axe from side to side, and burst out laughing. But Rigg was relieved to see a gleam of intelligence, a flicker of sanity, in the fighter's sleepless and swollen eyes.

"I see the camp is well guarded tonight," Ivar growled. "The woman is awake and her whelp has returned from the woods. Welcome back to the lair, young Rigg! Now I am ready to hear your story."

# The *Skraelings*

Rolf built a small fire on the beach. They sat around it, facing one another. Ivar leaned his huge axe on a piece of driftwood and bent forward to listen. The chieftain seemed calm, Rigg noticed, almost thoughtful, but his eyes revealed the instability in the man's soul, and his expression veered crazily from eager interest to disdain and fearful preoccupation.

Ivar was clearly a man obsessed, and as Rigg took this in, he began to grow doubtful that his tale could change much in the leader's heart. Nonetheless, he recounted what had happened in the woods with honesty and some gusto. The Vikings loved stories, and here was one that was new and strange.

As Rigg spoke, the night wore on, the sky lightened, and mist in great rolling waves hid the face of the long fjord. In the distance the high hills thrust up through the shimmering white blanket, gulls hovered in the solemn heavens, small fish jumped in the lagoon beyond the *knarr*, and frogs croaked from the marshes that rimmed the inner waters.

Rigg finished his tale, and there was silence. Ivar bowed his head as if in serious thought. Then, with a look at his mother, the boy reaffirmed his convictions that, despite what had happened to Helgi, they must trade peacefully with the red men, that they must take a cargo of wood and furs over to Greenland in the new *knarr*, find Leif, and receive their orders from him.

Ivar at first said nothing, then he reached over and pulled his axe toward him. Rigg held his breath.

"So the whelp is now the wise man," the chieftain spoke at last, and with bitter irony. "He can assure us these beings who paint their faces red and kill Vikings are peaceful souls, monks perhaps of the deep woods. That's why they captured you and Tyrkir, shot arrows at you, and have pursued you to our camp. Let me tell you, young one, that if we stay here it will be a matter of kill or be killed. These are wood savages and not human beings, and a true Viking would scorn to do anything but exterminate them."

Rigg recoiled in horror at this vehemence. A crazy look had come into the chieftain's eyes. He stood up, muttered to himself, and rubbed the blade of his axe gently against his bearskin coat, as if he were already cleaning it of blood.

"We're not going to trade with these people," Ivar said. "This is a frightening place—a hateful country—and we must sail as soon as possible. If they attack us, we'll fight them. I want badly to avenge our brave Helgi..." The chieftain paused, his voice dropping almost to a whisper. "Helgi's spirit has become a *sending*. You didn't know that, did you? Yet I have met it in my dreams. I blame Tyrkir for this. He is the only one with the power to raise a *sending*. And now he must call back the ghoulish thing, he must free my mind of it, or he will never sail on my *knarr*. I'll leave him here with your red men, whom you defend to me. We'll see how kind they are to him when the Viking swords leave this country."

Fianna murmured a protest, and Rigg jumped to his feet and started to speak. But Ivar raised his axe menacingly and growled, "Woman, shut your mouth and go fetch the rune master. *His* sleep is peaceful and he has had enough of it. Now he must clear my dreams of the demons he has unleashed on me...or else suffer the consequences."

Fianna got up, but she made no move to obey the chieftain. Rolf took her arm, fixed his gaze on the leader, and said quietly, "Ivar, I'm sorry about your bad dreams, but Tyrkir is a rune master. His magic is of the soul and not evil, and he is surely not responsible. I'll fetch him for you and we'll settle this matter at once. But remember, Tyrkir is Leif's old companion—and this boy's teacher."

Ivar seemed taken aback by these pointed words. Frozen in his tracks, he appeared incapable of speech or movement, but his eyes were full of hatred.

Rigg stood beside his mother and Rolf. A wild thought possessed him. Was it possible that he could wrestle the axe away from the chieftain?

At that moment several loud cries sounded from points all around the camp. The horn signal followed, ominously clear, from the high hills. Rigg sprang toward the scaffolding that supported the new *knarr*, climbed up, and peered across the lagoon at the heights around them. Four or five sentries were running at full speed toward the camp, shouting and pointing behind them.

"The attack!" Ivar bellowed as the horn sounded again and cry succeeded cry. "Your red friends are attacking us. Thor defend us! Now we'll taste blood!"

"Look, in the fjord, they're coming there!" Rolf shouted.

In the glimmering dawn a dozen canoes had slipped out of the mist and were running straight toward the beach. Scores of tribesmen sat upright in these boats and paddled easily through the light surf.

"Back to the main booth, you fools!" Ivar roared. "We'll be cut off if we stay here."

Rigg, who had twisted around to look at the canoes, now turned his gaze inland. A swarm of native warriors appeared on the hilltops. Down they came past the deserted guard posts, tall men, many of them carrying spears, as well as bows and arrows. They moved unhurriedly, as if they were strolling along to a feast or a ceremony, but to Rigg this made their advance all the more terrifying.

He scrambled down from his perch and joined the others. Ivar was already running headlong toward the main booth. Fianna looked doubtfully at Rolf.

"Someone must guard the new *knarr*," the navigator told them. "I'll stay. You two go with Ivar. Try to restrain him. No one has attacked us yet!"

Fianna threw her arms around Rolf. She hesitated for a moment, then took her son's outstretched hand to hurry along the beach after Ivar.

Morning, like the first dawn, seemed to explode around them. Figures ran in and out of the buildings. Everyone was in motion, shouting contradictory orders. On the hillside the red men advanced slowly, like a tide, making not a sound as they approached.

Half-dressed, the Owl ran from the main booth and greeted the chieftain. "I heard the alarm! It's the demon men!"

Big Thrand trudged after him, rubbing his sleepy eyes with a huge fist. "Demons? Who spoke of demons?"

At that moment Silk Beard sprinted in, the first of the guards to reach the camp. He was out of breath and his face was pale with fear. "Hundreds of them," he gasped. "Can't we get to the ship?"

Ragnar and Ulf, their doublets torn and ragged, appeared from the north post. "The demon men surrounded us," Ulf cried, waving his sword. "We started to fight our way through, and they opened a path for us."

"Red faces," Hedin muttered. "The boy told the truth."

"The weapons!" the Crow insisted. "Someone fetch shields and armour."

"Fifteen men, one boy, and a woman," Ivar muttered, "against a thousand warriors. The gods have not cast lots in our favour."

"Who says they are warriors?" a voice cut in. It was an old voice, a steady one, full of calm thought. The voice demanded attention—it was the rune master's. "Perhaps they have just come to get their boat," he said with a careless shrug. Tyrkir stepped out of the booth, wearing a bright red cloak, a gaudy piece of apparel that many of them had never seen before.

"This is no time to play the peacock," Ulf told him. "We need all your magic to get us out of this."

"That is why I am wearing this red cloak," the rune master told him. "There is magic in a colour sometimes."

"Foolish talk," Thrand grumbled. "Ragnar, come and help me fetch weapons and armour."

"Those devils are down on the beach, too," Ivar told them. "Rolf is on guard there. Pilgrim and Hauk, you go and join him. Eleven men here and three there—it's the best we can do."

"You'll count me as a man before the day is over," Rigg said with an angry gesture. "And Tyrkir, too!" He seized a sword with eager hands when Thrand and Ragnar carried them out.

"Form ranks in front of the booth!" Ivar ordered. "Crow and Ulf, man the bows. Shoot at their leader when I give the signal."

The chieftain stepped forward, his look ferocious. The men watched with awestruck glances. Then Ivar bent his head and mumbled some words. He had traded his axe for a sword, which he swung from side to side like a sinister pendulum. Within seconds it was as if he had lapsed into a kind of waking trance. His body swayed and he seemed about to launch himself into the air. *"No pain, no pain,"* he chanted softly. *"Kill them all!"*

"Our chief will save us," the Owl told them. But his own hands shook so that he dropped his sword twice, then held it fast against his breast, as if it were a magic wand.

Ivar stood glassy-eyed and shivering all over. He appeared to be in the grip of a fever as the men crowded around him. Thrand, however, noticed Fianna, standing tall but weaponless not far away. She had taken a position by the nearest shed, but still some paces in advance of their huddled ranks.

"Woman! Get back in the booth!" the Viking roared at her.

"Get back in the booth yourself, you old bellows! I'm an Irishwoman and the leman of Leif Eriksson. I'm standing with my son and Tyrkir."

Hearing these brave words, Rigg ran across to join his mother.

"Now the men are separated from the petticoats," Thrand sneered.

Rigg winced, and the anger stirred in him. He looked for Tyrkir, but the rune master had disappeared.

A small rise on the landward side protected the camp against the wind that sometimes roared down from the hills. Over this rise now, not a hundred and fifty feet from the embattled Viking warriors, appeared the red men. So silently, so effortlessly did they advance that they seemed to materialize from the earth itself. They did not turn or pause, but came steadily on, not in visibly ordered rows, but crowded together in a kind of living swarm. Without any spoken command, the intruders had formed a semicircle that effectively cut off the camp from the beach.

As they came nearer, Rigg noticed again how much they resembled the Vikings. They were tall men, fair-skinned, as he knew, beneath the bright red paint, with lavish hair, dark or reddish-brown, and large dark eyes. Far from being naked, they wore, like the Vikings, a kind of kirtle or doublet, edged with fur and belted at the waist—also leggings and low leather shoes. Most carried long spears and bows and arrows, but a few men, in the centre of the band, bore what seemed to be oversized skin-wrapped bundles.

When they were only about fifty feet from the Viking band, the whole array of red men stopped together. There was a long pause. Rigg could see Ivar swaying on his feet, his lips moving silently, his sword swinging rhythmically. The other Vikings surrounded him, looking uneasy, and in some cases terrified. Crow and Ulf stood a little to the rear and peered at the band of red men. The two Vikings fingered their bows with some restlessness, and Rigg judged they were trying to decide which of the throng was the leader.

That designation seemed to fit the tallest of the interlopers, a man who stepped out just then from the ranks, one who looked as formidable in person as Thrand, and who carried a spear with several bannerlike objects affixed.

The man raised his hand, and Ivar shouted, "Steady!"

But nothing happened. Everything was silent; no one moved. Then, without warning, the red men sang out.

Rigg took a step back. He had never heard anything like it. An eerie, high-pitched wailing filled the air. It was something like the cry of animals in pain, something like the wind when it howls on a cold night through a deep cave. A cold, searing sound, evoking autumn's frosty days and bleak nights in the heart of winter. Was it a lament, or a greeting? Rigg could not say. Yet he listened and decided it was a beautiful sound, even though it froze his blood and made him swallow hard to keep control.

So it was all the more horrifying when, amid the memorable, the terrifying beauty of that din, Thrand raised his hand, laughed, and bellowed to all the Vikings, "Listen to them. Just listen to the screechers. *Skraelings*, that's what they are! A screeching band of savages. They're nothing but animals. The gods will thank us for killing every one of them."

# ᚾᛖᛏᚼᛋᛏᚱ�ᚲᛆᛏ
# Catastrophe

Thrand spoke his bitter words and the Vikings roared their approval. Rigg started to protest, but Fianna cried "No!" and pressed her son's hand in a tight grip. Then Tyrkir stepped out of the adjacent shed, a magnificent figure in a long, flowing bright red cloak.

There was an immediate stir in the ranks of the red men, a palpable movement, as if all the leaves on a great oak had been shaken by a sudden wind. At the same time cries broke out and continued, even when the chieftain with the long lance turned to his band and shouted something, perhaps a command that his men come to order.

Tyrkir, however, paused only for a second. He marched away from the Viking ranks and, with arms stretched wide, so that the cloak spread out like a banner, approached the red men. At the same time he raised a loud chant, singing out in a high-pitched, keening manner. His words—if they meant anything—were incomprehensible to Rigg, but they sounded eerily similar to the sounds of the red men's language he had overheard in their village.

The effect of this on the band of red men was extraordinary. Many shouted and pointed at the rune master, others laughed, some did impromptu dances, but most touched their painted cheeks and looked around dazedly, as if seeking an explanation for this wonder.

When Tyrkir came within a few feet of the red men, however, the sensation became a near riot, for with a few deft gestures the rune master slipped off his cloak, folded it quickly into a bundle and, with outstretched hands, offered it to their leader.

There was immediate and pervasive silence.

Rigg, too, held his breath. The Vikings shifted uneasily. Then the red men's chieftain turned and spoke a few words to the nearest of his warriors. A path opened among the throng, and two warriors emerged, carrying the large skin-wrapped bundles Rigg had noticed earlier. These they laid on the grass directly in front of Tyrkir. The chieftain pointed at the bundles, and the men, with a few strokes of their long knives, cut them open.

Stooping, the chieftain removed a black garment or cloth from its wrappings and offered it to the rune master, while Tyrkir, at the same moment, handed the chieftain the neatly folded red cloak. A shout of approval greeted this gesture. The Vikings, looking on, were at first silent. Then Thrand spoke up, and his voice was full of scorn. "*Trade!* The red devils want to trade with us."

"Watch out," Silk Beard chimed in. "It may be a trick."

"How can you trust a *skraeling*?" Ulf added.

"But it's *sable*," Rigg protested. "They've given us valuable sable for a worthless old cloak." Dismissing the suspicions of his fellow Vikings with a laugh and a wave of his hand, Rigg went forward to congratulate Tyrkir on his wonderful gesture.

"We have a few more red garments and some dyes we can put to use," Tyrkir told him. "These people have a fondness for that colour, or so it seems. Did you like the way I imitated some sounds in their language?"

The rune master looked very pleased with himself, and Rigg clapped him on the back. "You're really a wonder," he said.

Meanwhile the red men milled around, laughing and lining up to see the marvellous cloak. Some of them reached out and touched the rune master and Rigg, too, as if reassuring themselves that these strangers were human beings, after all.

Rigg in turn touched one or two of the red men on the shoulders in a friendly manner. Most of them were tall and sturdy, with large dark eyes and shoulder-length straight black hair. Apart from their painted faces, there was nothing alien about them. In Viking clothes and style they could have passed for a Viking, while Rigg knew that he himself, suitably dressed and painted, could have passed for one of them.

It was a strange feeling, mingling with the enemy, with the people he had first seen as devils, people who had trapped him in a pit and whom he had later battled at the village. Yet it was wonderful, too, a release of tension, and at that moment everything, the great fjord, the distant mountain peaks, the rolling hills, the woods, the brightening sky, seemed suddenly not only more familiar but more intimately present to him.

Rigg smiled. His mother was coming slowly forward, nodding encouragement, but the Viking warriors remained huddled by the booth. They spoke together quietly, standing with grim faces and casting doubtful looks in the direction of the red men. In the middle of this group stood Ivar, who seemed to have fallen into a daze or trance and to have lost the power of speech.

Halfway to where her son stood, Fianna, distracted by a new arrival, stopped, turned, and cried, "Rolf!"

The bald navigator appeared on the beach path and now approached them, raising his hands in an obvious gesture of reassurance. "They've taken their boat back but harmed nothing," he shouted. "The *knarr* is safe and they've gone out into the fjord."

Rigg and Tyrkir, who had been distracted and noticed nothing of this, detached themselves from the murmuring crowd of native warriors and moved to join him. At that moment Rigg noticed a young red man standing close by, watching him intently. There was something familiar about his face. Surely this was the boy he had wrestled with in the woods.

Rigg walked over and, after some hesitation, laid his arms gently on the boy's shoulders. The boy likewise placed his arms on Rigg's shoulders. They stood for a moment regarding each other. Rigg knew their stance was that of two wrestlers about to grapple, and he smiled. The other boy did not smile, but nodded gravely, then detached himself from Rigg's embrace and walked away.

The red men were now walking easily and confidently around the booth, seeming to notice everything, touching the walls of the buildings, the scattered tools, even the Vikings' clothing and weapons—all with obvious delight, while commenting to one another, pointing and nodding at every new discovery.

The Viking warriors, Rigg saw, were reacting variously to the new situation. Their defensive formation had dissolved and one or two warriors, the Owl and Ragnar in particular, seemed amused and even relaxed in the presence of the red men. Thrand, however, had backed up against the wall of the carpentry shed, near the Viking smithy, and beside him stood Ivar, his sword held stiffly in his right hand, his eyes staring straight ahead, as if he were gazing into the heart of some void unperceived by the others.

"We must get Thrand and Ivar into the booth," the rune master whispered to Rigg.

Tyrkir's tone was urgent, and the boy felt a sudden twinge of fear. He looked around and saw the scene before him in a new light. Men mingled and milled around, strangers from different worlds trying to come to terms with one another. Suddenly Rigg saw the fragility of this fraternal moment. Without a common language, the two sides remained incomprehensible to each other, and everything depended on a kind of groping goodwill. The busy scene made Rigg think of strangers dancing and roughhousing together on the edge of a precipice.

Rolf did not see this. He turned to the others with a smile and declared, "These people will surely not harm us."

"Thanks to the rune master," Fianna said. She, too, seemed confident, even relaxed, and embraced all three men in turn.

The four walked slowly toward the entrance to the booth, where some red men were already peering in, as if working up courage to enter. Then Tyrkir cried out. His face had gone ashen, and Rigg, full of apprehension, followed the rune master's glance.

A smiling red man had approached Thrand and Ivar where they stood beside the tiny shed. Thrand looked on grimly as the interloper touched first his dark green cloak, then his helmet, and finally the spear clenched tightly in his beefy fist. Undaunted, the red man reached toward Ivar who, without warning, sprang to one side, swung his sword once and, with a single stroke cut, off the man's head. Then Thrand ran forward and speared one of the red men who stood beside the booth entrance. The warrior fell with a fearful cry, and silence ensued—the longest and most terrible moment of Rigg's life.

Then the native chieftain, sounding a war cry, ran forward. Ulf, standing in the shadow of the Viking booth, shot him in the throat with an arrow.

Everything was chaos.

Ivar had gone berserk. Howling like a wild animal, he ran among the red men, hacking and chopping, cutting

down men as they fled or cowered away before his
onslaught. Rigg ran about with Tyrkir, trying to stop the
melee, while Rolf pulled Fianna toward the booth
entrance.

The red men now rallied a little. Four or five warriors
had surrounded Thrand, and a terrific fight was in
progress on the other side of the carpentry shed. Arrows
came flying as native archers set up in the rear and
began to enter the fray.

Nothing stopped Ivar. The berserker roamed through
the field with fierce strokes and bloodcurdling cries,
driving the red men back toward the foot of the hill.

Rigg knew that all was lost. He retreated with Tyrkir
to the booth entrance. Rolf came out carrying swords and
handed them to the Vikings who reached the entrance
without weapons. Most of the men appeared dazed. They
huddled together but did not attack, although Ulf kept
firing arrows at the retreating red men.

Fianna came out and took Rigg's hand. The boy
could not look at her. He had heard much about the
berserk rage in battle, but what he saw was far beyond
any telling.

Ivar was no longer Ivar, but an animated body of
fury, bent on destroying everything in his path. His
shrill cry drove the red men back, and every warrior
who approached him was struck down. Already the
Viking chieftain had been speared in one shoulder while
two long arrows had lodged in his back. Yet he pressed
on, unrelenting, until at last he began to weary a little
and the red men gathered in a group of six or seven to
charge him.

Under their assault, made with long spears, he gave
some ground. Then a torrent of arrows engulfed him. He
staggered back, a hideous sight, stuck all over with the
quivering shafts. Confused, he circled blindly, stumbled
over the gift offering the red men had left lying in the
field, and fell. The native fighters came upon the Viking

chieftain and skewered him to the ground with their spears.

Thrand killed the last of his tormentors and ran forward. He was greeted with a torrent of arrows that stopped him in his tracks. He swayed like a great tree, then a warrior ran up and drove a spear through his chest. He started to topple, but the spear pinned him grotesquely where he stood. Another red man came up and slit his throat.

The native warriors gazed at the two fallen Vikings with close attention. Were they surprised at their power of death over these violent strangers? With blank faces they turned and fled up the hill after their retreating fellows.

For some time Rigg watched as the whole band of red men disappeared over the rise.

The Vikings stood stunned and uncertain. A few uttered mournful prayers, some peered doubtfully up the hillside, others sought the shelter of the booth. Rigg looked out over the field of the slain: bodies were strewn here and there in the grass, lying between the buildings and in the space around the unclaimed gift offerings.

*So this was a battle. This was the brutality of mankind.* No longer concerned about his manhood, Rigg buried his face in his hands and wept.

ᛏᛉᛅᛁ ᛚᛇᛁᛏ ᚠᛁᛅᛁ
# The Lost Land

All day the Vikings watched the hillside in terror. They dragged the bodies of the fallen red men, thirteen of them, up the slope and left them there. Rigg had taken an anxious look at the faces of the dead, but his companion of the night vigil was not among them.

The vultures arrived, then the crows, and the birds began their work.

Meanwhile Rolf, who was leader now, set the best craftsmen to finishing the *knarr*. They could have it ready to sail in twenty-hours, they told him. To Rigg and Fianna he said privately, "Pray to the gods that we're in time."

They placed the body of their dead leader and that of Thrand on separate rafts and floated them out into the bay. The planks were set on fire, and Tyrkir invoked Odin, the soul gatherer, to see them safely into the other world.

As evening came, the Vikings' terror increased. No one would take a hill watch, and Rolf decided they would set up their defences around the ship. Big fires were built there, and everyone, except the two sentries,

Ulf and Ragnar, who watched beside the booth door, settled down on the beach.

Very few slept that night. Rigg lay awake, listening to the sounds in the darkness, convinced the cries he heard were not made by birds or animals, but were signals preceding the inevitable attack. He was stunned by the thought that his closeness to this land had been severed, probably forever, by the violence of the previous day. He felt uprooted, sad, and already an exile. But as much as he had hated the violence he had witnessed, he vowed to die fighting beside Rolf, if need be, to save Fianna.

Fianna herself was busy and very cheerful, and Tyrkir was reassuring. "They will come back in order to kill us," he said. "But if they celebrate some funeral rites over their dead, we may gain enough time. My fear is that they will come by sea and blockade us on that side." Hearing this, Rolf sent the Owl out in a small boat to keep watch on the bay.

Dawn came without incident, and the Vikings were cheered a little. Then Ragnar reported that all the slain red men had been removed from the hillside. Their bodies had vanished, and there were no revealing tracks in the turf. The removal had been accomplished in the middle of the night, and in complete silence, and the Vikings once again fell into a state of terror. They felt as if an invisible enemy were playing cat-and-mouse with them and might strike when they least expected.

That day the work on the *knarr* took precedence over everything. The smithy, which they guarded the whole time, was a busy place. Some iron rivets still had to be made and driven into the lapstraked hull of the ship. One plank was laid over another and the planks lashed to the ribs with willow twigs shoved through the cleats. The final sewing was yet to be done on the square sail, and this kept Fianna busy. Tyrkir spoke to Rolf about a special dye. Of the big oars, each about sixteen feet long, they had two to finish. The rudder, or steerboard, still had no hole in the blade, and this was required to secure the rope that would fetch it up in shallow water. They had already fashioned the rigging out of the walrus hide they had been stocking all summer, and the anchor had been forged first of all, since Ivar had a belief that it was lucky to do so.

By the end of the day, most of these things had been done, and they were able to float the ship to test it and make sure they could trust it on the high seas. There was no question of stopping along the shore for repairs—that would mean exposing themselves to the vengeance of the red men. No one knew what messages might pass up the coast or what enemies might lie in wait for them farther on. The sooner they made it to the open ocean the better, for there the native boats would be no match for them, or so they thought.

When they realized they needed another morning to complete the loading of the vessel—even with minimum cargo—some of them were in despair.

"They're bound to attack tonight," Ragnar told the assembled Vikings. "We must sleep on the ship and sail away if they come after us."

Rolf agreed this was good plan. Then the Owl came rowing in and reported there were many war canoes assembled at the far end of the fjord.

The men exchanged grim glances. Rigg walked up the beach and tried to recover his equilibrium. He kicked at the stones and peered far down the fjord where the canoes must be lurking close in to the steep cliffs. The boy shook his head in frustration. He did not hate the red men, although he knew they would kill him if they could. For the first time he blamed Leif for putting them in this predicament.

Fianna walked up the beach and joined him. For a while they did not speak. Rigg tossed a few pebbles into the water and then said to his mother without looking at her, "Where is Leif? Why has he left us here?"

Fianna took his arm and steered him back to where the ship was anchored. "Leif is alive. I'm sure of it. Tyrkir read the runes just now and has found *Dagaz*. That's the rune of day, the breakthrough rune. I think we'll get out of here tomorrow. And Leif is not dead but, as always, distracted and busy with something new. You and I will have many good days with him yet."

"But how can I face my father when I've failed him so badly?" Rigg complained. All his doubts came pouring out. "I was the one who first saw the red man and thought he was a demon. It might have been better to have left it so! Tyrkir and I proved that the red men were human, but they followed us here and look at the result! Thirteen of them dead and our two best fighters gone with them. A crazy slaughter that never should have happened. I caused it, and I had no power to stop it. I looked on like a helpless child. And now I simply follow the others and sail away in fear. How can I explain this to Leif? Mother, I'm ashamed of what I've done here...and I wanted so badly to make things right!"

Fianna listened, then embraced her son and said quietly, "What you did was a miracle. You went into the dark woods, and when Tyrkir was captured you rescued him. Without that there would have been no possibility of friendship between the Vikings and the red men. It wasn't you who made Ivar a berserker or Thrand a bully! They chose the way of violence."

She withdrew a little. From her brooch chain she plucked a familiar object. It was a much-used spindle whorl, made of soapstone and taken from one of her old spinning wheels. Rigg had seen it bobbing up and down many times on the spindle as his mother made clothes or sails. Now she bent over, dug out some of the sand with her fingers, and set the implement there.

"I'll leave it behind," she said, "as a sign that we brought more than violence to this land. Someday perhaps you'll return and find it. By then you'll be a great man and you'll understand what you've accomplished here and be proud of it." She covered the half-buried spindle whorl with sand. "Until a better time," she whispered.

A burden seemed to lift from Rigg's shoulders as he watched his mother bury the spindle whorl. When she was finished, they walked back to where the *knarr* lay at anchor.

That night all the Vikings slept on the ship. They woke in darkness to find the booth in flames. Luckily they had removed many of their possessions and some supplies of food and stowed them on the beach. When dawn came, they loaded these and prepared to bid farewell to the land that had seemed to be theirs but that was now lost to them.

They rowed the *knarr* out into the bay, and Rolf scanned the length of the fjord. "They're waiting for us there. I'm sure of it," he announced. "We'll not get out of here without a fight."

After another hour's rowing, they had run three miles down the passage. Here the fjord narrowed and bare cliffs rose on either shore. Mountains towered in the distance. Dangerous reefs abounded, and there were many little bays where the enemy might lurk. Behind them, at their camp, the booth still smouldered in the sunlight.

The Vikings said very little. The rune master kept watch with Rigg and Fianna, and none of them seemed surprised when a small flotilla of canoes emerged from a nearby bay and drove toward them.

"Raise the square sail!" Rolf commanded, and with much shouting and groaning by the crew who worked it, the sail went up. It was a beautiful creation, dyed not with common blue or green but bright red—an idea of Tyrkir's that Rolf, against his will, had agreed to. To the Vikings the colour red meant violence and battle, and the men had had enough of that on the fatal day that saw the death of their best fighters.

The wind was light but favourable and the sail filled up. The men shipped oars and the vessel leaped ahead. It rode well in the water and everything seemed to be in fine trim.

The native canoes had paddled to within fifty yards of the ship. There were about thirty of them, and they approached in two squadrons on either side of the Vikings, but as soon as the red sail went up, a shout arose from the attackers and the canoes veered away and ran tiny circles on both port and starboard sides.

"Red is a magic colour to them," the rune master explained. "I only wish I could tell what they are thinking now."

The men in the canoes shouted and waved their arms, but the Viking ship sprinted between the two waves of attackers and made its way up the channel toward the far end of the fjord and the open sea beyond. The canoes came on in the wake of the Viking ship, but fell slowly, inevitably, behind. At one point, however, they had been close enough for Rigg to think he had once again recognized the young red man, his double of the midnight watch. He raised an arm in salute and farewell, but the other, if indeed it was he, only watched him without making any gesture.

"A good ship!" Rolf shouted then to the rune master. "And we forgot to give her a proper name."

"Call her *Ehwaz*, the horse," Tyrkir suggested, "for she rides the sea like a fine steed gallops across a field."

As the newly dubbed ship *Ehwaz* coasted on, Rigg stood in the stern and saw the native boats dwindle and the land recede. The little space of the shore the Vikings had occupied had also sunk out of sight. Visible everywhere were deep forests, towering hills, and the long line of the stern, rocky coast. Beyond all of these, Rigg knew, was still an unfathomed country and mysteries to be encountered by those bold enough to venture beyond the coast.

Strange peoples had come here long before and had long since departed. They were ghosts now and fugitives, as the Vikings soon would be, visitors who had left hardly a mark on this new country. Who would remember their coming and going? Who would care?

And yet, as Rigg realized, as Fianna had reminded him, much had happened to him here, and he had done much, accomplished a few feats that future sagas might tell about. This new land, disappearing now minute by minute before his eyes, had changed his life forever. For one thing, it had given him a deeper sense of both the beauty and the cruelty of the world he inhabited.

Rigg turned and saw Fianna and Tyrkir in conversation, watching him. They smiled approvingly, and he smiled back at them, set his glance on the open sea, and made a vow to come back to Vinland—and if that proved impossible—to meet with his best strength whatever future the gods had decreed for him.